The Baby-sitter III

She grabbed the receiver. "Hello?"

"*Hi Babes.*" A low, whispered voice.

"Mark? Is that you? I can't hear you very well."

The voice was dry, like the crackling of dead leaves, and sounded as if it were coming from far away. Debra had to struggle to hear the words. And when she heard them, she felt her entire body go cold with terror:

"*I'm alive. I'm back. Company's coming, Babes.*"

Classic Point Horror never dies...

Point Horror

The Baby-sitter III

R. L. STINE

SCHOLASTIC

Scholastic Children's Books,
Commonwealth House,
1-19 New Oxford Street,
London, WC1A 1NU, UK
A division of Scholastic Ltd
London ~ New York ~ Toronto ~ Sydney ~ Auckland
Mexico City ~ New Delhi ~ Hong Kong

First published in the USA by Scholastic Inc., 1993
First published in the UK by Scholastic Ltd, 1994

This edition published by Scholastic Ltd, 2002

The Baby-sitter III

Chapter 1

Mr. Larson smiled at Jenny Jeffers. "The two most important rules at The Doughnut Hole," he said, rubbing his chin, "are: Don't Touch and Don't Eat. No free samples."

Jenny stared back at him. "You mean, no free samples for the customers?" she asked hesitantly.

Mr. Larson chuckled, as if she had cracked a joke. He shook his pudgy head. "No free samples for *you*! If our workers started scarfing down our doughnuts, pretty soon they wouldn't fit behind the counter. Take a look. There's not much room back here."

Jenny let her eyes roam down the long yellow counter. A woman and a little boy were seated at the far end. The boy had smeared a chocolate doughnut over most of his face. The woman was frantically trying to clean him up with a napkin.

The large yellow-and-red neon sign, sus-
pended from the ceiling, was reflected in the
long window that ran the length of the restaurant. Jenny read the words *THE DOUGHNUT
HOLE* backwards in the glass. Outside the
window, she could see people hurrying up and
down the wide corridor of the mall.

I don't really want to work in a doughnut
shop this summer, Jenny thought wistfully. It's
going to be really boring. And I don't like Mr.
Larson. His face is so pale and doughy, just
like his doughnuts.

"So do you want the job?" he asked, wiping
a round coffee stain off the counter with a damp
cloth.

No. No. No, Jenny thought.

"What is the pay again?" she asked.

"Four dollars an hour."

"Yes. I'll take it," Jenny said softly.

Her mother had just been laid off from her
job as a legal secretary. Jenny had no choice.
She had to work this summer. They really
needed the money.

"When can you start?" Mr. Larson tossed
the wet cloth under the counter. An elderly
couple, dressed in identical navy-blue running
suits, entered the restaurant and stood staring
at the display of doughnuts.

"Monday, I guess," Jenny told him. "School is out. So I guess Monday."

"Be here at six-thirty sharp. We open at seven. We do a big breakfast business."

What a summer, Jenny thought unhappily. Staring at a wall of greasy doughnuts at six-thirty every morning.

"Fine," she said, forcing a smile.

Mr. Larson reached out and shook her hand. His hand felt warm and squishy, like a jelly doughnut.

Jenny pushed open the glass door and escaped into the crowded mall. As she walked past The Doughnut Hole, she glanced back through the glass in time to see Mr. Larson stuff an entire chocolate cruller into his mouth.

Jenny had to laugh. No wonder Mr. Larson was beginning to resemble a doughnut!

Still chuckling, she walked away quickly, dodging a baby stroller, nearly colliding with a boy on Rollerblades.

Jenny's thoughts were on the summer. It won't be a lot of fun, she thought. But at least I've got a job. Mom will be happy.

She sighed as she continued down the crowded mall corridor. The job, she realized, didn't pay much better than baby-sitting.

Baby-sitting.

The word still made Jenny shudder and feel cold all over.

She'd had such horrifying experiences as a baby-sitter. She knew she'd never baby-sit again.

It was nearly two years later, and she still thought about it all the time. Two years later, and she still thought about Mr. Hagen, the man who hated baby-sitters. Jenny was the baby-sitter for the Hagens. Until Mr. Hagen had tried to kill her.

But she had lived. And he had died.

Died because of her. . . .

Dr. Schindler — he was Jenny's psychiatrist — said she was doing really well.

But Jenny wasn't so sure.

Why did she still think about Mr. Hagen so much? Why did she still dream about him? About the night he tried to push her over the edge of the rock quarry and instead went hurtling to his own death? Why did every blond little boy remind her of Donny Hagen, his son?

Wasn't it time she forgot all that had happened?

"Jenny! Hey — Jenny!" A hand grabbed Jenny's shoulder.

Startled, she spun around to find her best friends Claire and Rick grinning at her. "Didn't you hear us calling you?" Claire asked.

"No. I . . . uh . . . was thinking about something," Jenny replied. "How's it going? What are you guys doing?"

"Just hanging out," Rick said, placing a hand on Claire's shoulder. He shrugged his broad shoulders and flashed Jenny his goofy grin.

Rick was a big, good-looking teddy bear of a guy, with dark eyes that always seemed to be laughing and curly black hair that he seldom brushed. He was wearing faded jeans, torn at both knees, and a red-and-black T-shirt with the words *METAL MANIACS* emblazoned across the chest.

Claire was tall and thin, an inch or two taller than Rick, with straight brown hair swept back in a ponytail and serious brown eyes. She wasn't really pretty, but would be some day. She was wearing an enormous yellow T-shirt over black leggings.

"We were too late for the movie, so we're wandering around," Claire said. "You shopping?"

"No." Jenny shook her head. "I just had a summer job interview. At The Doughnut Hole."

"Are you going to be a doughnut?" Rick joked.

Claire shoved him away. "That was really lame, you know?"

Rick laughed. "Yeah. I know."

"I got the job," Jenny said without enthusiasm.

"Hey, that's great," Claire started. Then seeing Jenny's downcast expression, she added, "Isn't it?"

"Well . . . I need a job," Jenny replied, shoving her hands into her jeans pockets. "Dr. Schindler thinks it's a good idea for me to get out of the house and do something different this summer. And, of course, with Mom being laid off, we really need the money."

"And the free doughnuts!" Rick added with a grin.

Jenny shook her head. "No free samples," she said, imitating Mr. Larson's stern voice.

"No free samples? You should quit!" Rick declared.

Claire glared at him. "Give Jenny a break." Claire didn't like to kid around. She was a serious, caring person, and seldom made jokes. Rick was an unlikely boyfriend for Claire. He was always cracking jokes, seldom serious.

Claire turned to Jenny. "You're lucky to get a job. Most places aren't hiring this summer."

"Yeah, I know," Jenny replied quietly. She tugged a strand of dark hair off her forehead. "I'm working the morning shift, so at least I'll be free at night to see Cal."

"Does Cal have a job yet?" Rick asked.

Jenny shook her head. "Not yet."

Claire glanced at the clock over the entrance to Sutton's, the largest department store at the mall. "We have time before the next show. Come on — walk around with us."

"Okay. Good," Jenny replied, smiling. "I promised Mom I'd get the car home. But I have a little time."

"I'm just going to grab a cone at Mulligan's," Rick said, starting across the aisle toward the ice cream parlor. "Can I get you anything?"

"No thanks," Claire and Jenny replied in unison.

Claire stopped to stare at the display in a shoe store window.

A bathing suit in Sutton's window caught Jenny's eye, and she moved close to admire it.

I won't be needing a bathing suit this summer, she thought wistfully. Not at The Doughnut Hole.

When she turned away from the window, she saw him.

And froze.

He was walking toward her. A large man in a yellow windbreaker.

She saw the red face. The close-cropped brown hair.

And those eyes. Those steel-gray eyes.

Mr. Hagen.

It's Mr. Hagen, Jenny realized, gaping at the approaching figure in horror.

But he's *dead.*

I know he's *dead.*

He's dead, and he's here, walking toward me.

And what was that in his hands?

Jenny pressed her back against the window glass and stared open-mouthed.

He was carrying a baby.

Mr. Hagen — dead Mr. Hagen — was carrying a baby in his arms.

And as he drew near, he raised his steel-gray eyes to Jenny's.

His expression was blank, as blank as death.

And with a quick, simple motion, he grabbed the baby's head with one hand, twisted it, and pulled it off.

Chapter 2

Jenny didn't realize she was screaming until Claire grabbed her shoulders.

"Jenny — stop! Jenny, what *is* it?" Claire cried.

Jenny's entire body convulsed in a shudder of terror.

"Jenny, what's *wrong?*"

Mr. Hagen gaped at her, his ruddy face twisted in surprise. He still held the baby's head in one hand, its torso cradled under his other arm.

Only it wasn't Mr. Hagen.

It was another man, Jenny saw.

Another big, red-faced man. Not Mr. Hagen.

"Jenny — are you all right?" Claire demanded, holding onto Jenny's shoulders.

"What's going on?" Rick cried, pushing his way through the crowd that had gathered. He had a double-dip chocolate cone raised in one hand.

"Is she okay?" the red-faced man asked Claire, keeping his distance, his eyes studying Jenny.

"The . . . the b-baby — " Jenny stammered, pointing with a trembling hand.

Bewildered, the man held up the baby's head. "This?"

It was a doll, Jenny saw.

Not a baby. A doll.

"I'm taking it back to the toy store," the man told her. "The head comes off."

"A doll," Jenny said weakly.

"Are you okay?" Claire asked Jenny.

"Yeah. I guess." Jenny nodded. She raised her eyes to the man. "Sorry." Her legs felt shaky. The lights shimmered. The crowd around her started to blur.

She closed her eyes.

When she opened them, the man was gone. Claire and Rick stood beside her, their faces filled with concern. "I thought — " Jenny started to explain. "I saw him pull off the head, and I thought — "

"It was a very real-looking doll," Claire said softly, glancing at Rick.

Rick's ice cream was dripping down over the cone. He licked the chocolate off the back of his hand. "Should we take you home?" he asked.

"I — I've always had a wild imagination," Jenny said unsteadily. "I guess this time I . . ." Her voice trailed off.

"Let Rick and me drive you home," Claire said tenderly.

"Thanks," Jenny replied. "My car is that way." She pointed.

When am I going to stop seeing Mr. Hagen everywhere? she asked herself, allowing them to lead her to the parking lot. Mr. Hagen is dead. He's been dead nearly two years.

When am I going to stop thinking about him?

When?

Jenny stared at herself in her dressing table mirror. I should wash my hair, she thought, straightening her wavy, brown hair with one hand.

I look terrible.

Her dark eyes were red-rimmed and bloodshot. Her normally creamy skin looked rough and blotchy.

She hadn't slept much the night before. She'd had another nightmare about Donny and Mr. Hagen, which had startled her awake at two in the morning. She'd felt edgy and irritable all day.

And now, seeing how dreadful she looked wasn't cheering Jenny up at all.

"Good news!" Mrs. Jeffers' voice broke through Jenny's glum thoughts.

She turned away from the dressing table to see her mother rush into the room, an excited smile on her face.

"You got a new job?" Jenny asked, climbing to her feet.

"No." Mrs. Jeffers bit her lower lip. "It's not about me. It's about you." She plopped down on the edge of Jenny's unmade bed.

"What's the good news?" Jenny asked, walking over to the bed and staring down at her mother. Mom really should do something about all that gray hair, Jenny thought.

"You've been invited to spend the summer with your cousin Debra," Mrs. Jeffers announced. She stared at Jenny expectantly, waiting for a happy reaction.

But all Jenny could manage was a "Huh?"

"I arranged it all with your Aunt Julia. A change of scenery will do you so much good, Jenny. It's so beautiful upstate. And you and Debra have always gotten along so well."

"But, Mom — we discussed this yesterday. I have a job for the summer," Jenny protested. "And Dr. Schindler — "

"I spoke to him about it this morning," Mrs.

Jeffers interrupted. "He thinks a change of scenery will be good for you, too."

"Well, thanks to both of you for deciding my life," Jenny snapped. "Behind my back!"

"Jenny — " Mrs. Jeffers climbed to her feet and confronted her daughter face-to-face. "We all want what's best for you, dear." She sighed. "I don't want you to go away for the summer. I'll miss you. I'll be terribly lonely. But I really think it'll be good for you to be away from here."

Jenny uttered an exasperated sigh, but didn't reply. Crossing her arms over her chest, she glared harshly at her mother.

"Jenny, sit down for a while and think about it," Mrs. Jeffers urged. "You had another nightmare last night, didn't you?"

"Maybe," Jenny replied grudgingly.

"And you thought you saw Mr. Hagen two nights ago at the Walker Mall?"

"Yeah. Well. . . ." Jenny turned away from her mother. "Am I on trial here or something?" she asked shrilly.

"Of course not," her mother replied, obviously stung by the accusation. She tried to put a comforting hand on Jenny's shoulder, but Jenny pulled out of her reach.

"Mom, listen, I appreciate what you're doing, but — " Jenny stopped in midsentence, startled by the sadness she saw on her mother's face.

Mom looks so much older, so much grayer, Jenny realized, studying her mother intently. Is it because of me?

"If you stay with your cousin, you won't have to work at The Doughnut Hole," Mrs. Jeffers continued, not giving up. "I know you weren't exactly looking forward to working there all summer, Jenny."

"How do *you* know? Maybe I'm planning a *career* in doughnuts!" Jenny declared. She had started out angry, but the absurdity of this idea made her burst out laughing.

Before they realized it, Jenny and her mother were both laughing out loud and hugging each other.

"I thought you liked Debra," Mrs. Jeffers said finally, wiping tears of laughter from her eyes with her fingers.

"I do," Jenny replied. "She's a little too perfect, though. With that perfect figure. And that perfect little face. And that perfect blonde hair."

"She's very pretty," Mrs. Jeffers agreed softly.

"And she can be very competitive," Jenny added. "She always has to win, always has to get her way."

"I guess we don't know someone else who's like that," Mrs. Jeffers said pointedly, teasing Jenny.

Jenny didn't react. She suddenly remembered Cal. "Cal and I, we planned to spend a lot of time together this summer," she said, more to herself than her mother.

"I'm sure Cal will understand," Mrs. Jeffers said. "He's worried about you, too." She glanced at herself in the dressing table mirror, then turned back to Jenny. "And maybe he can come visit you upstate."

"Yeah. Maybe," Jenny replied thoughtfully.

"So you'll go?" Mrs. Jeffers asked, bending to straighten the blanket on Jenny's bed. "Shall I call Aunt Julia?"

"I guess," Jenny said, forcing a smile. "Thanks, Mom."

A pleased grin spread across her mother's face, momentarily smoothing away the wrinkles. She crossed the room and hugged Jenny happily. "I'll miss you," she whispered.

Jenny was thinking about Cal. How would he react to this news?

She never knew how Cal would react. They had been going together for several months, but in many ways, he remained a mystery to her.

For one thing, he was so quiet. It was hard

to know what he was thinking. And he had a dark side, an angry side that he tried to keep from Jenny.

But Cal had been very understanding, very caring. And when the nightmares kept coming, when Jenny had thought she was being pursued by Mr. Hagen from beyond the grave, Cal had been there for her.

Leaning over the dressing table, she brushed her dark hair. Then she pulled a long-sleeved white sweater over her T-shirt. She took a last glance at herself, fretting about how pale she looked, then headed downstairs.

"Are you going out?" her mother called from the living room.

"I'm going over to Cal's," Jenny called to her, picking up the car keys from the table in the front hallway. "I don't want to tell him over the phone."

"Don't stay too late," Mrs. Jeffers warned. She said something else, but Jenny was already out the door.

It was a cool night for June. Wind gusts shivered the fresh leaves on the trees. The sky was red-tinged and starless, threatening rain.

With a shudder, Jenny slid onto the cold car seat and pulled the car door shut. She dropped her bag onto the passenger seat and pulled the seat belt over her chest.

She started to turn the key in the ignition, then stopped.

What was that shadow sliding across the side of the garage?

Was it a man?

She held her breath, staring hard through the windshield.

Was someone there?

No. No one.

Trees bent in the gusting wind. The late tulips by the front porch bobbed and trembled.

No one there.

Just my imagination again, Jenny thought, starting to breathe. Every shadow scares me.

I think someone is hiding in every shadow.

I really *do* have to get away from here.

Feeling jittery, she backed down the driveway and drove across town to Cal's house. She parked at the curb across the street from his house and cut the lights. Then, pushing open the door, she climbed out and, leaning on the car door, took a deep breath, trying to steady herself.

She stared down the block of small, box-shaped houses.

Cal's block is so dark, she thought. The streetlights were all out. The houses were black shadows against the red-gray sky.

Turning her eyes to Cal's house, she saw

orange light in an upstairs window. Cal must be up in his room, she thought.

She had started to cross the street when she heard footsteps behind her.

Hurried footsteps.

With a silent gasp, she started to jog.

The footsteps behind her moved faster.

This wasn't a shadow, she knew.

This wasn't her imagination.

Someone was chasing her.

Chapter 3

Jenny's sneakers slapped the dark driveway as she ran. She gasped for air. Her chest throbbed with pain.

"Hey — !" A breathless voice behind her. "Hey — !"

She heard gruff wheezing at her ankles. An animal sound.

"Hey — stop!" The breathless voice, pleading.

"Oh!" Jenny cried. The animal uttered a low grunt and darted in front of her, blocking her path.

It was a dog, she saw. A small terrier.

Jenny wheeled around to face her pursuer. "What do you want?" The words burst out of her in a shrill voice she didn't recognize.

The man stopped a few yards behind her, breathing heavily. He was middle-aged, maybe fifty or so, very overweight and balding, dressed in baggy shorts and a big sweatshirt. He held up her bag. "You dropped this."

"Oh." Jenny felt the blood rushing to her head, felt her face grow hot. "I — I'm sorry. You scared me," she said.

"I was walking Petey," the man said, pointing to the terrier who was sniffing the side of the stoop. "I saw you drop your bag when you got out of the car." He blew out a long breath. "Whew! Quite a chase!"

"I'm really sorry," Jenny told him, taking the bag from his hand. "It — it's so dark. I heard someone behind me, and — "

The man chuckled. "I guess Petey and I look like pretty desperate characters."

"No. I — I just got scared," Jenny explained. "I'm really sorry. Thanks. I mean, for the bag."

The man said good night and coaxed the dog away from the stoop. Jenny watched them disappear around the corner.

What am I going to do? she thought, ringing Cal's doorbell with a trembling hand.

I'm turning into a total nut case!

The porch light flashed on. The door opened. Cal's pale blue eyes went wide in surprise. "Jenny — hi!"

He pushed open the screen door to let her in. His spiky blond hair looked almost platinum in the white porch light. The gold stud in his ear caught the light and gleamed for a moment.

Jenny followed him into the dark living room. He clicked on a table lamp and turned to face her, his expression questioning. He was wearing a pale blue T-shirt over wrinkled tan shorts. He was barefoot.

"My parents went to bed early," he said softly, gesturing toward their room in back. "I was just listening to some music."

"I — I had to talk to you," Jenny told him, avoiding his stare. She sat down on the arm of the worn, brown leather couch. "I didn't want to do it over the phone."

His blue eyes locked on hers. The light caught the scar along the bottom of his chin. "What's going on?" he asked warily.

"Change of plans," she said softly.

She told him she was going to stay with her cousin upstate for the summer. At first, he didn't seem to react. He stared at her blankly with his pale blue eyes, rubbing the scar under his chin.

"Maybe I'll come with you," he said finally, dropping down on the couch and taking her hand. "I mean, I don't have a job yet. I could go with you and look for a summer job up there. Then we could be together."

Jenny squeezed his hand. "You know your

parents wouldn't let you do that," she said softly.

"Sure they would," he insisted. "They don't care what I do."

Jenny shook her head. "I — I've been so messed up, Cal. I really need a total change." She paused, watching his expression change to disappointment. "I'll be back in September," she whispered. "Then we can have fun catching up on all the good times we missed during the summer."

He let go of her hand and climbed to his feet. Then he walked slowly to the window and stared out at the darkness.

He's hurt, Jenny thought. He's really hurt.

He stared out into the dark night, leaning with both hands on the windowsill.

"Well . . . aren't you going to say anything?" she demanded finally.

She could see the muscles in his jaw tighten. "What's there to say?" he muttered bitterly. "You've already made up your mind. You're ruining our summer."

He's acting tough, Jenny thought, staring at his hard, cold expression. He doesn't want me to see how hurt he is. So he's acting hard and tough.

Or *is* he acting?

Staring across the room at him, she realized

she didn't know Cal very well. In fact, Jenny realized with a shudder, she didn't know him at all.

"Hi," Debra Jeffers whispered, "is this Terry?" She was lying on her back in her bed, the cordless phone cradled between her shoulder and chin.

"Yeah. Who's this?" Terry replied suspiciously on the other end of the line.

"Don't you know who it is?" Debra whispered, teasing. She giggled.

"No. Who is it?" Terry asked impatiently.

Debra could picture the bewildered look on his face as he tried to identify his mystery caller. She could imagine his green eyes narrowed in concentration, the little freckles flaring on his cheeks.

He's so cute, she thought.

"I've been watching you, Terry," she whispered sexily. "From afar."

"Come on," he groaned. "Give me a break. Is this Loren?"

Debra giggled. "No, Terry. Guess again."

"What do you want? I've got to go mow the lawn," he said.

"What do I want? I want *you!*" Debra whispered.

"Huh?"

"I want you, Terry."

"Who *is* this?" he demanded.

"Your secret admirer. Come on. Can't you guess?"

Silence.

"Don't you want to get to know me, Terry?" Debra teased.

He cleared his throat. "Do you want to go out or something?" he asked in a low voice.

"Do *you?*" Debra whispered.

"I guess," he replied reluctantly. "But who is this?"

"It's me," Debra whispered.

"Who's me?"

"I told you. I'm your secret admirer." She pushed herself up on the bed, crossing her long legs, staring up at her bedroom ceiling.

"Listen. I've got to go," Terry said.

"Don't go. I'll miss you, Terry," Debra teased.

"Do you . . . uh . . . want to go out tonight?" Terry asked.

Debra giggled. "What do you like to do at night, Terry?"

"Huh?"

"What would you like to do with *me* tonight?"

He snickered. "Whoever you are, you have a very sexy voice."

"Thank you, Terry," Debra whispered. "You do, too. Your voice really turns me on."

There was a long pause. "So do you want to go out?"

"I can't," she told him.

"Huh? Why not?"

"Because then I wouldn't be a secret admirer anymore, would I!"

Debra hung up and tossed the phone beside her on the bed.

Thinking about how confused Terry must be, she laughed out loud.

But her laughter was cut short when she saw the shadowy figure looming in the doorway.

"You!" Debra cried angrily, scrambling to her feet. "What are *you* doing here?"

Chapter 4

The figure stepped out of the shadows. He stared at Debra in silence, his expression blank.

"Don — what are you doing here?" Debra demanded. Glaring at him angrily, she tossed her long blonde hair back over her shoulder with one hand.

"I want to talk to you," he replied, returning her stare.

He's so big, she thought. So powerfully built. Don was on the wrestling team at school. He worked out all the time.

It was one of the things that had attracted her to him the previous fall. She had never gone out with a real jock before.

He was wearing maroon sweats. His short, brown hair appeared wet, as if he had just showered.

He took another few steps toward her. His

expression turned menacing. His round, dark eyes burned into hers.

She felt a shudder of fear, but held her ground. "Who let you in? How long have you been standing there spying on me?" she demanded.

"Long enough." He picked up a small stuffed dog from her dressertop and examined it.

"Put that down," Debra snapped. "Get out of here, Don."

"I just want to talk," he said, shuffling the dog from hand to hand.

His hands are so big, he could crush that stuffed animal, Debra thought.

"There's nothing to talk about," she said coldly. She walked over and grabbed the stuffed dog from his hands.

His dark eyes narrowed in hurt. "No harm in talking, is there?"

"Don, please," Debra pleaded impatiently. "I really want you to leave. We broke up, okay? You're a great guy, but I don't want to go out with you anymore."

"But, Deb — "

"And I don't want you barging into my house, haunting me all the time." She tossed her long hair back again. It was constantly falling over her face, and she was constantly brushing it back over her shoulders.

"You're cold," Don said, his handsome face reddening. He shook his head. "You're really cold, Debra."

" 'Bye-'bye," she replied, motioning to the door.

"Maybe I'll tell Terry how cold you are," Don said, picking up another stuffed dog from her dressertop collection.

"Terry? What about Terry?" Debra snapped.

A dark grin spread across Don's face. "Maybe I'll tell Terry who his secret admirer is." He snickered.

"You mind your own business," Debra said sharply. "Just get out of my life, okay?"

"Maybe I'll tell Mark, too," Don threatened, tossing the dog from hand to hand. "Maybe I'll tell your boyfriend Mark how you like to call Terry at night and whisper to him over the phone."

"You pig!" Debra screamed angrily. She could feel herself losing control, but couldn't stop herself.

She had broken up with Don two weeks ago when school let out. What right did he have to be in her bedroom, listening to her private conversations, threatening to tell Mark, threatening to spoil her summer — out of childish spite?

"Get *out!*" she screamed, and threw the stuffed dog at him.

It bounced off his broad chest.

Don laughed. He strode forward and grabbed Debra's arm.

Then, with surprising strength, he pulled her to him, nearly lifting her off her feet.

He pushed his mouth against hers in a desperate kiss.

"Let go!" She struggled to free herself, pulling back with all her strength.

He laughed again, his dark eyes wild with excitement.

His hand tightened around her arm as he pulled her close again. "Debra, please — "

"Let go!" Debra shrieked. "Don — stop! Stop — you're *hurting* me! What are you going to do?"

Chapter 5

"Don — stop!"

Debra struggled to squirm out of his grasp, but he was too strong.

"Hey — what's going on?" a voice called from the doorway.

Startled, Don released Debra and spun around.

"Jenny — !" Debra cried, grateful for the intrusion.

"I'm all unpacked," Jenny said, staring at Don. "I heard voices and — "

"This is Don. He was just leaving," Debra said brusquely, rubbing her arm where Don had gripped it.

"Hi," Don said to Jenny, embarrassed, his face bright red. "You're Debra's cousin?"

"Yes. Jenny Jeffers," Jenny told him, casting Debra a questioning glance.

"Same last name. As Debra," Don said awk-

wardly. He turned to Debra. "Hey, sorry. I
didn't mean to hurt you or anything. I was
just — "

" 'Bye," Debra said coldly. "Don't call me.
I'll call you."

Don, his face still tomato-red, started to say
something, but stopped. He shook his head re-
gretfully, then turned and hurried from the
room, the floorboards groaning under his heavy
footsteps.

"What a creep," Debra declared after she
and Jenny heard the front door slam behind
him. "I can't believe I went out with him for
the whole school year."

"Was he hurting you?" Jenny asked, con-
cerned. "I heard you shouting and — "

"Don's just a big animal," Debra said, rubbing her arm. "But he's harmless." She snickered. "And he's history. He won't be coming
back."

"The last time I was here, you were going
with a little skinny guy named David," Jenny
said. She bent to pick up a stuffed dog from
the rug.

"That's old news," Debra told her, tossing
back her hair. "Skinny David was at least three
boyfriends ago."

"I'm impressed," Jenny said, and laughed.

"You'll like Mark," Debra said, taking the

stuffed dog and returning it to its place on the dressertop. "I've been going with him since I dumped Don. He's a great guy. You'll meet him later."

"I will?" Jenny asked.

Debra started to reply, but her mother appeared in the doorway. "Jenny, do you need anything? Can I help you unpack? Is your room okay? I love that top."

"This? It's just from the Gap," Jenny said.

Debra's mother, Julia Jeffers, always talked a mile a minute. She never asked one question when it was possible to ask three. She was a pretty, energetic woman, young-looking, with a boyish figure, her blonde hair cut in a short bob. She wore a blue Lycra tanktop over black leggings.

"We haven't seen you for so long," Mrs. Jeffers said, turning Debra's desk chair around and sitting on it backwards. "How long has it been? Two years? Longer? I really can't remember."

"More than a year," Jenny replied. "But you look exactly the same, Aunt Julia."

"Bull," Mrs. Jeffers replied. But she was obviously pleased by the compliment.

"To answer your questions," Jenny continued, "the room is perfect, and I unpacked all my stuff."

"You don't need more hangers?" Debra's mother asked, leaning her chin on the back of the desk chair. "Another blanket, maybe? No. You won't need another blanket. That room gets pretty hot. It's in the sun all day. In fact, maybe we should get you a fan. I'll ask Carl about it. Did you call your mother?"

Jenny nodded. "Yeah. I called her before I unpacked." She turned to Debra. "It was really nice of you to invite me. I mean — "

"We really wanted you to come," Mrs. Jeffers offered before Debra could reply. "You and Debra have always gotten along so well. And since neither of you have brothers or sisters, you only have each other. You can be sisters all summer."

"Mom — !" Debra looked embarrassed.

"Well, when your mother said you needed a change of scenery," Mrs. Jeffers continued, ignoring Debra's protest, "I told her right away she should send you up here. Get some good fresh air. Meet a lot of new friends. You'll forget your problems soon enough."

"Thanks, Aunt Julia. I know it's going to be great," Jenny said sincerely.

A breeze fluttered the curtains in front of the open window. Jenny jumped, startled by the sudden movement.

Debra chuckled. "Ghosts," she joked.

"I can see you're a bundle of nerves," Mrs. Jeffers said to Jenny. "Your mother was right. You do need a change."

"I — yes. I do," Jenny replied awkwardly.

Debra glanced at the desk clock. "Oh, wow!" she exclaimed, jumping up. "It's nearly eight. I'm going to be late."

"You promised Mrs. Wagner you'd be prompt," Debra's mother scolded. She climbed to her feet and pushed the desk chair back under the desk. "Better hurry. You taking Jenny with you?"

"Yeah. Sure," Debra replied. She moved to the mirror and hurriedly started to brush out her hair.

"Have a good time," Mrs. Jeffers said, flashing Jenny a warm smile. "I'll be up when you get back. Carl and I always stay up very late." She started out the door, then returned to give Jenny a long hug. "I'm so glad you're here," she said. Then she hurried downstairs.

"Where are we going? What are you almost late for?" Jenny asked, turning to Debra.

Debra was busily applying lip gloss to her mouth. "To my job."

"Huh? You have a job?"

"Yeah." Debra nodded, staring at Jenny's reflection in the mirror. "But it's no problem. You can come with me."

"What kind of job?" Jenny asked. She moved beside Debra and started to straighten her own hair.

"Baby-sitting," Debra replied.

"Huh?" Jenny froze.

"I baby-sit this adorable baby three nights a week," Debra told her. "Just a couple of blocks from here. Wait till you see him. He's the cutest thing."

"Well, I don't know . . ." Jenny said reluctantly. She suddenly felt cold all over. Her knees were trembling. Her heart was thudding.

"Come on." Debra turned out the dressing table light and took Jenny's arm. She started to tug her to the door. "The baby sleeps the whole time. It's perfect. You and I can talk for hours, really catch up on things."

"But, Debra — "

"Jenny, come on," Debra urged. "It'll be fun."

Chapter 6

"Your mom is really great," Jenny said.

"She drives me crazy," Debra replied. "She asks a million questions and then doesn't wait for an answer. She talks so fast, you can't remember which question you're answering!"

Jenny laughed.

"My poor dad can never get a word in," Debra continued heatedly. "I don't remember what his voice sounds like!"

"Well, I still think she's terrific," Jenny insisted. "She's been so nice to me."

Debra scowled. "She likes you. But wait till she gets to know you!"

Jenny laughed.

They were walking the three blocks to Mrs. Wagner's house. It was a warm night. A pale half moon floated low over the roofs of the houses. The air smelled fresh and sweet.

It felt good to be walking with Debra, talking, walking through a new neighborhood. Maybe Mom was right, Jenny thought. Maybe a change of scene was just what I needed.

"You and your mom get along, don't you?" Jenny asked, watching a station wagon filled with kids roll by slowly.

"Most of the time," Debra replied. "But she's just in my face too much. I mean . . ." She paused, debating whether or not to finish what she had started to say. Then she continued in a whisper, "That's why I told her I baby-sit *three* nights a week."

Jenny stopped at the curb, her mouth open in surprise. "Huh? You mean you *don't* work three nights?"

Debra shook her head. Her blonde hair caught the pale moonlight. Her eyes lit up mischievously. "No. Only two nights. On the third night I go out with Mark. My mom doesn't really approve of Mark. Do you believe it?"

"How come?" Jenny asked.

They crossed the street. The houses on the next block were older, Jenny saw. And larger. With wide, tree-filled front lawns bordered by tall, carefully trimmed hedges.

"No good reason," Debra replied with some bitterness. "He got in trouble in school last year. A cheating thing. No big deal. It wasn't even Mark's idea."

"And so your mom — "

"She says he has a flawed character," Debra replied, frowning. And then she added angrily, "Well — who doesn't?"

"Aren't you afraid of getting caught?" Jenny asked, watching a fat jack rabbit scamper across the sidewalk and disappear into a hedge. "I mean, on the night you're supposed to be baby-sitting?"

Debra didn't answer at first. Then she muttered, "I really don't care."

A car rolled past slowly. The driver, a teenager with long hair, leaned his head out the window and grinned at them. "Hey, how's it going?" he called over the blare of heavy metal guitars from his car radio. "Need a lift?"

"Not from you!" Debra called.

The car squealed away with a burst of speed.

"Do you know him?" Jenny asked.

"No," Debra replied. "But I didn't like his car."

They both laughed.

"There's Mrs. Wagner's house," Debra said, pointing.

Jenny gazed up at the long, ramshackle house, redbrick with tall, shuttered windows. The hedge along the front had grown wild, over the sidewalk. The lawn looked as if it hadn't been mowed in weeks. Tall weeds poked up everywhere.

Debra caught the surprised expression on Jenny's face. "Mrs. Wagner and her husband were divorced a few months ago," she explained. "I don't think she's had much time to think about taking care of the yard."

The two girls made their way up the driveway, their sneakers crunching over the gravel.

Jenny suddenly felt all of her muscles tense. She had a heavy feeling in the pit of her stomach. Her throat tightened.

She took a deep breath and held it.

I'm not the baby-sitter, she told herself. There's nothing to be afraid of.

Debra is the baby-sitter.

I'm just here to keep her company.

Nothing is going to happen. Nothing *can* happen.

She let her breath out slowly. Her heart was pounding. The heavy feeling in her stomach refused to leave. Her legs felt as if they weighed a thousand pounds as she followed Debra onto the front stoop.

The front door opened before Debra had a chance to knock.

"Hi, Debra. You're late," Mrs. Wagner said fretfully. She pushed open the screen door. The top of the screen was torn. It flapped loose from the frame.

"Sorry," Debra said quickly. "This is my cousin Jenny. She's visiting for the summer."

"Hi, Jenny," Mrs. Wagner said, biting her lower lip, studying Jenny quickly with her eyes.

Jenny suddenly realized she was still holding her breath. She let it out with a burst. "Nice to meet you," she choked out.

I don't want to be here, she thought, looking around the cluttered living room.

I don't want to baby-sit.

Something terrible will happen.

Something even more terrible than before will happen.

You're not the baby-sitter! she reminded herself. *Debra is the baby-sitter. Everything will be okay.*

Mrs. Wagner strode quickly to a low table and began shuffling through a bulging briefcase. "Got to make sure my assignment is here," she said. "I can't go to class without my assignment. Oh. Here it is."

Jenny stood awkwardly in the living room doorway, watching Mrs. Wagner. She was a thin, birdlike woman with a short mop of curly black hair, streaked with gray. Her green eyes darted nervously. She continued to bite her lower lip anxiously as she closed up the briefcase.

She wore black leggings that emphasized her skinny legs, and an oversized white shirt.

"You'd think I was going to Harvard or Yale instead of the community college," she said, straightening the collar of her shirt in the front entryway mirror. "But I do want to do well in this course."

She tucked the briefcase under her arm and turned to Debra. "Don't get married too early," she told her. "That's what I did. I never got to finish college. So now I have to do it two nights a week." She headed to the front door.

"Is Peter asleep?" Debra called after her.

"Oh. Peter. Of course. Yes." Mrs. Wagner shook her head. "I'm so nervous about this class, I forgot all about Peter. I'm a great mom, huh?"

"That's okay, Mrs. Wagner," Debra said, making her way to the stairs. "I'll go up and take a look at him. Don't worry. Peter's never any trouble at all."

"See you in a few hours," Mrs. Wagner said, and disappeared out the door. The screen door closed quietly behind her.

Debra turned to Jenny, a grin on her face. "She's a little nervous."

"I guess!" Jenny replied. "Let's go up and see Peter."

The baby was snoring softly, lying on his stomach. He had a mop of curly black hair, like his mother.

"He's a good sleeper," Debra whispered, reaching over the side of the crib to straighten his light blanket. "Usually he doesn't wake up at all when I'm here."

"What an easy job," Jenny whispered back.

They tiptoed back downstairs, got Cokes from the refrigerator, and settled down across from each other in big living room armchairs.

Jenny gazed around the room. The furniture was big and comfortable-looking. But every surface — the tabletops, the bookshelves, the window ledges — was cluttered with objects of all kinds: small glass vases, porcelain figurines, tiny picture frames with old photographs inside them, china eggs, miniature soldiers, painted thimbles.

"I guess Mrs. Wagner is a collector," Jenny said, picking up a tiny china pitcher. It felt cool and smooth in her hand.

"Do you believe all this *stuff*?" Debra replied, shaking her head. Then she startled Jenny by jumping to her feet, nearly knocking over an end table filled with tiny animal figurines. "The signal! I almost forgot!"

"Huh? What signal?"

Debra hurried out of the room. She returned a few seconds later. "I had to make sure the porch light was on. That's our signal. If the light is on, Mark knows it's safe to come in."

Jenny set down her Coke can. "Mark? He's coming here?"

"Yeah. He usually comes about half an hour after Mrs. Wagner leaves. Unless the porch light is off." Debra took a long sip of Coke. "You'll like Mark. He's really great," she said, tossing her hair behind her shoulders.

A loud click, probably the refrigerator turning on in the kitchen, made Jenny jump. "Sorry," she told Debra. "I — I'm a little jumpy. I mean, baby-sitting. You know."

Debra gasped. "Oh, Jenny. I'm so sorry. I completely forgot — "

Jenny shook her head and forced a smile. "No. I'll be okay. Really. I — I have to get over this. I can't just live in constant fear, you know?"

Debra studied her face. "I never really heard the whole story," she said softly. "I mean, about what happened to you. Can you talk about it? Is it hard for you?"

Jenny's hand tightened around the Coke can.

She tucked her legs under her on the chair cushion. She cleared her throat. "There isn't much to tell, really."

"I know you went through something terrible," Debra said, staring down at a worn spot in the carpet.

"Yeah. Terrible," Jenny repeated. "I had a job, see. Baby-sitting for this family. The Hagens. They had this really cute little boy. Donny." Jenny sighed.

"Listen, if you don't want to tell me . . ." Debra started.

"After I baby-sat for Donny for a while, I started getting these frightening phone calls," Jenny continued, staring hard at the red-and-white can until it became a blur. "A whispered voice saying, *'Are you all alone, Babes? Company's coming.'*"

"Yuck," Debra said, pulling up her legs and sitting sideways in the big armchair.

"There had been all these attacks on baby-sitters all over town." Jenny continued. "And here I was, getting these frightening calls, getting these threats. And then . . . and then . . ."

She took a deep breath. "It turned out that Mr. Hagen, Donny's dad, he was the one making the calls. He was the one attacking the baby-sitters."

"But why?" Debra asked.

"He and his wife had a baby. And the baby died when a baby-sitter was taking care of it. And I guess Mr. Hagen just freaked. He started murdering baby-sitters all over town."

"I don't believe it!" Debra cried with a shiver. "It — it's like a horror movie."

Jenny nodded. She realized her hands were shaking. She set the Coke can down on the end table. "No one knew who was attacking the baby-sitters. The police couldn't catch the guy. But one night I figured out it was Mr. Hagen," she told Debra, speaking in a low whisper. "That night, I thought he was driving me home. But he knew that I knew. He drove me to this deserted rock quarry outside of town. A deep hole with nothing but rocks down below. He backed me up to the edge."

"He was going to push you over the side?" Debra cried, her face pale with horror. She tugged at a strand of blonde hair, twisting it in her fingers.

"Yes," Jenny said. She cleared her throat again. "He came running to me to push me over. But I ducked. He — he sailed over the edge. He fell. Onto the rocks. I — I heard his body crack. It sounded just like an egg cracking. I can still hear that sound. Still."

"Wow," Debra exclaimed, tugging at her

hair. "Wow." She raised her eyes to Jenny. "He was killed?"

Jenny nodded. "I know it wasn't really my fault. I mean, Mr. Hagen was evil. He was a crazy, evil man. He deserved to die. But I can't stop thinking about him. I can't stop thinking it was my fault."

"But he was a killer, Jenny," Debra said. "You have to keep telling yourself that. You can't feel guilty. He was a killer."

"After Mr. Hagen died, I started getting calls from him," Jenny revealed. "The same threats. The same whispered threats: *'Company's coming, Babes.'*"

Debra sat up. Her mouth dropped open. "What do you mean? How could you get calls from him after he died?"

"I was baby-sitting for another family," Jenny explained. "A little boy named Eli. And the calls started. The threats started. I — I really thought Mr. Hagen had come back. That he was back from the grave. Or that maybe he really hadn't died at all. I — I started having these frightening nightmares about him coming back, coming back to get me. I still have them."

Debra shuddered. "You poor thing. But he was definitely dead, right?"

Jenny nodded. "It was someone else. It was my doctor's assistant. She was jealous of me.

So she pretended to be Mr. Hagen. She made the frightening calls. She frightened me so much. It was so cruel. So cruel."

"That is really *sick!*" Debra exclaimed.

"I've been seeing Dr. Schindler for nearly two years," Jenny revealed, shifting her position in the big chair. "He says I'm doing really well, making a lot of progress. But I'm not so sure." Her voice trailed off. She stared down at the carpet.

"Why? What's wrong?" Debra asked.

"I still have the nightmares," Jenny replied. "I still dream about Mr. Hagen. I still see him pulling himself up from his grave, half-decayed, chunks of skin falling off his face."

"Wow," Debra muttered, twisting her hair around her finger, staring sympathetically at her cousin.

"And I think I see him wherever I go," Jenny admitted. She shuddered. She tried to continue, but no sound came out. She took a long drink from the Coke can.

"Maybe I shouldn't have brought you here," Debra said thoughtfully. "Maybe baby-sitting brings back too many horrible memories for you."

"No. I'll be okay," Jenny assured her. "It's good for me, I think. I mean, I should face my fears. I guess. It's just that . . ." She sighed.

"Just what?" Debra asked softly.

"I have this weird feeling," Jenny replied after a while. "This sick feeling that Mr. Hagen *is* still alive. That's why I can't stop dreaming about him. Seeing him. Because he *is* still alive. He *is* going to come for me."

"Jenny, no," Debra said. She climbed to her feet and moved next to Jenny's chair. She put a comforting hand on Jenny's shoulder. "You saw him die, Jenny. He's dead. That's it. You have to stop thinking like that. You have to stop thinking about this creep Mr. Hagen. You have to put it all behind you."

"I — I don't think I can," Jenny confessed.

Another noise in the kitchen made them both jump. Debra squeezed Jenny's shoulder.

"What was that?" Debra whispered.

They froze, listening.

A scraping sound.

A creaking floorboard.

Footsteps.

A cough.

"Debra — someone's in the house," Jenny whispered.

Chapter 7

They both heard another harsh cough from the kitchen.

More scraping of shoes against the floor.

Jenny climbed to her feet, her features tight with fear. Debra stood beside her, still as a statue, listening hard.

"Is it Mark?" Jenny whispered.

Debra shook her head. "He wouldn't come in the back."

"Let's call the police," Jenny suggested, her voice a trembling whisper.

Debra swallowed hard, her eyes wide with terror. "The phone's in the kitchen."

"Huh?" Jenny reacted with shock. "Deb, there's got to be another phone."

"No. Mrs. Wagner had to cut back when her husband left."

Without realizing it, the girls had begun to make their way to the kitchen. Keeping against

the hallway wall, they crept silently, Debra
leading the way, their eyes on the yellow rectangle of light from the kitchen.

They stopped just outside the kitchen door.

Jenny leaned hard against the wall. She felt
dizzy. The floor had started to tilt. The flow-
ered hallway wallpaper became a shimmering
blur.

What am I doing here? she thought, closing
her eyes, trying to force her heart to stop thudding so hard in her chest.

Why am I baby-sitting again?

Why are frightening things happening to me
again?

When she opened her eyes, she saw that
Debra had stepped into the kitchen. "Who's
there?" Debra called loudly. "Who is it?" Her
voice trembled, revealing her fear.

Jenny took a hesitant step forward, determined to keep up with her cousin.

"Who's there?" Debra repeated shrilly.

"I'm back!" a strange voice replied.

Chapter 8

"He can't be back!"

Jenny wasn't sure whether she thought the words or screamed them.

"He can't be back! He's dead!"

Debra turned to stare at her. Her hands pressed against her face, Jenny stepped into the kitchen — and saw a large, brightly dressed woman staring back at her from the sink.

"I'm back," the woman repeated in a hoarse, throaty voice. She narrowed her dark eyes at the two startled girls, as if challenging them.

The woman appeared to Jenny to be somewhere between fifty and sixty. She was short and very fat. She wore an enormous, flower-patterned wraparound skirt and a bright yellow sweater. Her face was heavily made up, with heavy black eyebrows painted above her dark eyes, and thick red lipstick smeared over

51

her mouth. Her round cheeks were pink. She had raven-black hair pulled straight back into a long ponytail.

Standing at the sink, she carried a plain brown shopping bag in one pudgy hand. Her fingers were covered with sparkly rings, Jenny saw.

"I came back," she repeated, still squinting at Jenny and Debra, her expression menacing.

"Who *are* you?" Debra managed to say.

"Maggie," she replied. "And I haven't been drinking, if that's your next question."

"But how did you get in?" Debra asked, flashing a quick glance at Jenny.

Jenny located the wallphone beside the kitchen counter. It would be easy to reach it quickly, she decided, to call the police.

"I still have my key," Maggie said, a smile crossing her bright lips. "Mrs. Wagner forgot to take back my key."

Debra relaxed a little. "You work for Mrs. Wagner?"

"Used to," the woman said. She made a disgusted face. "I was the housekeeper. But I was . . . how do you say it? . . . let go."

"But you — " Debra started.

"I never drank during the day," Maggie interrupted, staring hard at Debra as if expecting her to challenge the statement. "And I certain'y never drank when I took care of little Peter."

Debra flashed another worried glance at Jenny.

"Things disappeared," Maggie said. She reached up her free hand and turned on the sink faucet, then quickly turned it off. "Things disappeared around here. Mrs. Wagner's husband disappeared, didn't he!" She threw back her head and laughed, a deep, throaty laugh. "Yeah. The husband disappeared. Then poor Maggie had to disappear."

She's crazy. Debra mouthed the words to Jenny.

Jenny nodded in reply, her expression troubled.

"Things disappeared certain'y. But I didn't disappear 'em," Maggie said with increasing anger. She turned the faucet on and off again. "I didn't disappear 'em, you hear?"

"Yes," Debra muttered, watching the woman turn the faucet on and off, on and off.

"You can't just turn Maggie off like a faucet," the woman said, saying each word slowly and distinctly.

Debra took a deep breath and stepped closer to Maggie. "Well, I'm the baby-sitter tonight," she said. "Can I help you or anything?"

"I'm only taking this bag," the woman said,

holding up the empty shopping bag. "I'm only taking what's certain'y mine."

"That's fine," Debra said shakily.

"Fine," Maggie repeated. "Fine, fine, fine!" The word sounded angrier with each repetition. "I'll tell *you* what's fine, young lady!" she shouted.

"Maggie, please — " Debra pleaded.

"Fine, fine, fine!" Maggie shook a fat fist at Debra. "I know what's fine and what's not. I certain'y never drank during the day."

"That's good," Debra said, her voice unsteady.

"Certain'y things disappeared. But I didn't disappear 'em. I didn't disappear Mr. Wagner!" Again, she had a hearty laugh at her private joke.

"Well, shall I tell Mrs. Wagner you were here?" Debra asked.

Maggie cut her laughter short. "I only came for what's mine." She held up the brown shopping bag. "That's all I want. What's mine. You can't turn Maggie off like a faucet. I want what's mine."

She started to the kitchen door, swaying heavily from side to side as she walked, folding the shopping bag under the arm of her yellow sweater.

"Well, good night," Debra called after her, relief in her voice.

Maggie turned at the door. Her eyes narrowed. Her expression turned hard. "Stay away from here!" she shouted, spitting the words.

"Huh?" Debra cried, startled by the woman's sudden threat.

"Stay away from here," Maggie repeated. "It isn't the place for you. Things disappear. You hear me? Things disappear."

The screen door slammed hard behind her.

As soon as she was gone, Debra slumped against the kitchen counter and collapsed in laughter. "Do you believe her?" she cried. "Do you believe her? And what was she wearing — a beach umbrella?"

"I thought she was kind of scary," Jenny said softly, her arms crossed over her chest. "She was so drunk."

"Drunk and crazy," Debra said, shaking her head.

"She seemed so angry," Jenny said thoughtfully, staring at the darkness beyond the screen door. "I mean, she was threatening us there before she left, wasn't she?"

"She's messed up," Debra said, shaking her head. "She's *way* messed up. We'll have to tell

Mrs. Wagner to get the locks changed."

With a shiver, Jenny started to make her way back toward the living room. "I was scared," she admitted. "Really scared."

"Me, too," Debra replied. "At first, anyway."

"I — I thought it was Mr. Hagen," Jenny confessed softly. "Isn't that awful? That was the first thing I thought. It's Mr. Hagen. He's back. He's followed me here." Her voice cracked with emotion. "Am I crazy, Debra? Am I totally crazy?"

"Of course not," Debra replied soothingly. "Just stop thinking about Mr. Hagen, Jenny. Tell yourself you're going to stop thinking about him. From this moment on."

"Yes. You're right. I have to do that," Jenny said uncertainly. "He's never coming back. Never."

And then both girls cried out in alarm at the sound of the heavy pounding on the front door.

Chapter 9

The knocking was repeated. Even louder.

Jenny stared at the door but didn't move.

Debra started to laugh. "It's only Mark," she said, putting a comforting hand on Jenny's shoulder. She hurried down the hall and pulled open the door.

"Hey, didn't you hear me knocking? I've been out here for ten minutes!" Mark declared. He pushed past Debra into the hallway, an annoyed frown on his face.

His expression turned to surprise when he saw Jenny. "Oh. Hi."

He was good-looking, Jenny instantly decided. He had wavy red-brown hair with sideburns that framed his slender face. He had obviously spent a lot of time outdoors, for he had a dark suntan, even though it was only June. The tan made his green eyes sparkle like emeralds. He wore faded blue denim jeans and a sleeveless navy-blue T-shirt.

"We were back in the kitchen. Why didn't you ring the bell?" Debra asked.

"You're Jenny — right?" Mark asked, ignoring Debra's question.

Jenny nodded. "Yes. Hi, Mark."

"I guess Debra has told you a lot about me," he said playfully. "Well, it's all true."

"I never mentioned your name," Debra said dryly. She punched his bare shoulder. "You're so tanned, you're disgusting."

"Hey, thanks," he replied, grabbing her hand before she could punch him again. "You're cute, too."

They wandered into the living room. Debra sat beside Mark on the couch. Jenny eased into the big armchair across from them, sliding her legs onto the arm. "How'd you get so tan?" she asked Mark.

"I'm a lifeguard," he told her. "At the community pool."

"All the twelve-year-old girls love him," Debra said, squeezing his hand. "They pretend to drown so Mark can save them."

"Do you save them?" Jenny asked, laughing.

"Only the cute ones," Mark replied.

"You're a pig," Debra told him, rolling her eyes. "A disgusting tanned pig."

"You're so nice tonight," Mark said sarcastically. He put his hands around Debra's throat and playfully pretended to strangle her.

"Is it a fun job?" Jenny asked when they stopped wrestling. "Being a lifeguard?"

"Kind of," Mark replied thoughtfully, scratching his chest through the blue T-shirt. "Mostly you just sit there. It's almost like watching TV. Except you get to blow a whistle a lot."

"Mark's very deep," Debra said sarcastically.

They all laughed. Debra snuggled against Mark.

"Wish I had a summer job," Jenny said wistfully.

Debra reacted with surprise. "You do? I thought you just wanted to chill out this summer."

"Not really," Jenny told her. "I had a job back home. Before you invited me to come here. I'm really going to need some money in the fall. You know. For clothes and school stuff. And with Mom laid off . . ."

"I'll bet my dad could get you a job," Mark offered. He slid his arm around Debra's shoulders.

"You do?" Jenny shifted in the chair, lowering her feet to the floor.

"Yeah," Mark told her. "Dad's best friend owns the riding stable up on Clearlake Road. He's always looking for helpers in the summer."

"You mean horseback riding teachers?" Jenny asked. "I used to be a good rider."

"No. Just helpers," Mark said. "You know. Wranglers, they call them. They get a lot of day campers up there. Little kids riding. They need people to help them up on their horses and show them how to put their feet in the stirrups. You know. Stuff like that."

"And people to catch them when they fall on their heads!" Debra joked.

Mark laughed and pulled Debra close. "You're sick," he said. "You're really sick."

"You say the sweetest things," Debra replied.

"I guess I could do that," Jenny told Mark with growing enthusiasm. "I mean, be a wrangler. That could be fun."

"I'll talk to my dad tomorrow," Mark promised. And then his eyes opened wide with surprise and he leapt to his feet as bright yellow headlights rolled up the living room wall.

They heard the rumble of a car outside.

"Mrs. Wagner is home early!" Mark declared.

"Quick — get *out* of here!" Debra cried, giving him a shove.

Mark stumbled over the low coffee table, knocking over several china knickknacks. "Ow!" he cried out, but kept running toward the back door.

Debra hurried to the large living room window and peered out.

"Won't Mrs. Wagner see his car?" Jenny asked.

"Wait!" Debra called. "Mark — wait!"

"Huh? What's wrong?" Mark's shout came from the kitchen.

"It's not her," Debra called. "It's just a car turning around in the drive." She laughed.

A few seconds later, Mark returned, rubbing the knee that had hit the table. "Heart attack time," he said breathlessly, grinning at Jenny.

"Does this happen often?" Jenny asked.

"Only once a night," Debra replied, motioning for Mark to come back to his place beside her on the couch.

Mark glanced at his watch. "I'll have to go soon. She'll be back in half an hour or so."

Debra pulled him close and they began kissing.

Jenny looked away. *Three's company*, she told herself.

But what was she supposed to do while they were making out?

She climbed out of the chair and explored the room, picking up china figurines, studying the dozens of snapshots in multicolored frames.

Debra and Mark have forgotten I'm here, she thought, rolling her eyes. She took a quick glance at them, totally entwined on the couch.

She decided to wander upstairs and take another look at Peter.

A few minutes later, Debra sighed and pulled her face from Mark's. She took a couple of breaths. Then, smiling, started to lean forward to kiss him again.

But Jenny's terrified scream made Debra pull back.

"Debra — help! Come quick! The baby — he isn't breathing!"

Chapter 10

"Debra — quick! *Please!*"

Jenny's shrill, terrified cry made Debra gasp. She pushed herself up and plunged toward the stairway, Mark right behind her.

This can't be happening, Debra thought, feeling sick.

It *can't!*

It seemed to take an eternity to climb the stairs. She reached the landing, panting loudly.

"Debra — the baby!"

Debra hesitated just outside the baby's door, swallowing hard. Then she burst into the room.

In the dim light from the nightlight on the floor, Debra saw Jenny huddled over the crib. Jenny looked up as Debra and Mark entered, her features twisted in horror, her chin trembling.

"He — he's — "

Debra took a deep breath, stepped up beside

Jenny, and bent over the crib. The baby was silent.

So deadly silent.

With a trembling hand, she touched his face. Still warm.

She slid her hands under his arms and lifted him up.

He opened his eyes.

He gurgled his surprise at being awakened.

"Oh!" Jenny sank back against the wall, her hands raised to her face. Debra could see that she was trembling all over.

"He's fine," Debra told her, her voice a trembling whisper.

"Oh, man!" Mark cried. "What a scare!" He sank to his knees.

"You're fine, aren't you, Peter?" Debra asked the baby, pressing her forehead against his. She held him against her for a long moment, then lowered him to his crib.

He made a few noises, then settled back to sleep.

Debra raised her eyes accusingly to Jenny.

"He — he was so quiet," Jenny stammered, tears rolling down her cheeks. "He'd been snoring before. But then he was so totally silent, and it's so dark in here, I — "

"Wow," Mark repeated, still on his knees on the shaggy carpet. "Wow."

Debra walked over to Jenny and put a comforting arm around her trembling shoulders. "You really *are* a nervous thing, aren't you," she said softly.

"I'm sorry," Jenny said. "I'm really sorry."

"No. I'm sorry," Debra replied, still holding her. "I forced you to come here tonight. I shouldn't have."

Jenny apologized again, wiping tears off her cheeks with her hands. "I — I really lost it, Debra. I feel so stupid."

"You were scared, that's all," Debra replied. She led the way back downstairs.

"I feel like a perfect jerk," Jenny muttered, shaking her head.

"Stop," Debra told her. "No one's perfect."

Jenny forced a smile. But her thoughts were dark and painful.

What's *wrong* with me? she wondered.

Will I *ever* get over this? Am I totally cracking up?

"Now, where *were* we?" Mark asked slyly, pulling Debra back to the couch.

But once again, headlights rolled up over the wallpaper.

"Mrs. Wagner!" Debra cried. " 'Bye, Mark!"

" 'Bye, guys!" Once again, Mark went flying to the kitchen.

Jenny checked her face in the hallway mirror, making sure she had wiped away all traces of tears.

The kitchen door slammed. The front door opened. Mrs. Wagner entered, carrying her bulging briefcase. "How'd it go, girls?" she asked.

"Just fine," Debra told her brightly. "No problem."

"Hey, this is great!" the boy said, grinning down at Jenny. He rustled the reins in front of him. His horse, a brown mare with white markings on its legs, brushed a fly off its hind quarters with a swish of its tail.

"Hold still," Jenny said. "Let me adjust the stirrups for you, Brad." She tugged the stirrup strap tighter, then slid the boy's foot into it. "How's that feel?" she asked.

"Perfect," Brad replied.

Jenny slapped some dust off the leg of her jeans, then smiled up at him. Just three days at this job, she thought, and already I'm a pro.

The horse snorted as if reading her thoughts.

"Just remember, Brad," Jenny instructed, leading the horse over to the others in Brad's day camp group, "pull back hard on the reins, and your horse will stop. But as soon as she stops, stop tugging. Or else the horse will think you want to back up. Got it?"

"Got it," Brad assured her. He called to a friend, "Hey, look — this is easy!" The horse walked slowly over the dusty path. "What's my horse's name?" the boy called back to Jenny.

"Pockets," she shouted.

"Pockets?"

Jenny watched him pull back on the reins. The horse obediently stopped. He's a cute kid, she thought.

She untied another horse, a black gelding, from the hitching post. "Who's next?" she called.

A timid-looking girl with long, copper-colored hair stepped forward slowly.

"Come on," Jenny beckoned encouragingly. "I've got a nice, gentle horse for you."

A few minutes later, the twelve kids in the day camp group and their counselor were riding off on the dirt trail that led through the woods, their horses loping slowly, a riding instructor in the front and one at the rear.

Jenny watched until they disappeared into the trees. Then she started to the stable to get a water bucket.

"Hey, how's it going?" A voice right behind her.

Jenny turned to see Gary Killeen smiling at her. He wiped his forehead with the red bandanna he wore around his neck. Then he replaced his battered black Stetson hat on his head.

Gary was nineteen or twenty. He was a real wrangler. From Jackson Hole, Wyoming.

He wasn't exactly handsome, but Jenny liked the way he looked. He had thick, golden eyebrows that looked like big caterpillars under his cowboy hat. His eyes were steely gray, narrow and close together. He had a great smile, Jenny thought, with two front teeth that jutted out at odd angles.

"I'm doing great," she told him, slowing her pace so he could catch up with her. He had been really friendly to her since her first day, and had shown her a lot about saddles and stirrups and the other equipment.

"The kids really seem to like you," Gary said, lowering the brim of his hat.

"Well, I used to . . . uh . . . be a baby-sitter," she told him.

"I used to be a baby," he said, grinning at her, his gray eyes lighting up under the thick, blond eyebrows.

He has a weird sense of humor, she thought.

"Not too busy today," she said. They stepped into the shade of the stable. Jenny took a deep breath. The air smelled of hay and horse sweat.

"Busy enough," Gary replied. "We got another camp group this afternoon."

"How many?" Jenny asked, filling the water bucket.

"Fourteen, I think." Gary stood with his hands on the hips of his straight-legged jeans, admiring her as if she were a prize stallion.

Jenny could feel herself blushing. "I'll help you saddle up the horses," she offered.

"You *bet* you will!" he exclaimed, chuckling. "You know, you're not a bad-looking filly yourself," he said, lowering his eyes to his boots.

"Thanks. I guess," Jenny replied awkwardly. She hoisted the bucket, water slopping over the sides. "I've got to go water Betsy and Jedediah."

"Who *names* these horses?" Gary exclaimed, shaking his head.

Jenny tended to Betsy and Jedediah. The horses seemed so tranquil, standing under the hot sun, chewing at some grass, waiting for their next assignment.

Jenny stroked Betsy's mane for a while. The horse uttered a low whinny in appreciation, then kept on pulling up slender weeds from the dirt.

When she returned the bucket to the stable, she looked for Gary. But he had disappeared. Probably in the small office behind the stable.

It was so quiet, so calm.

Jenny leaned against the rail fence in front

of the stable, staring out at the green woods, waiting for the day camp group to return.

After a while, she found herself thinking about Cal. He had promised he'd write. But she'd been up here more than a week, and hadn't heard a word from him.

I wonder what he's doing right this minute, she thought. I wonder if he's thinking about me. I wonder if he found a job. I wonder if he's going to come up here to visit me.

Maybe I'll phone him tonight, she thought.

Debra popped into her mind. The night before, Debra had been playing one of her telephone pranks. She had called a boy named Terry and whispered sexy things to him, telling him she was his secret admirer.

Jenny listened in on an extension. Terry got all tongue-tied and then tried to persuade his "secret admirer" to go out with him. Debra hung up on him while he was still talking.

Jenny thought the whole thing was kind of cruel, but she and Debra giggled the rest of the night about it.

Debra admitted she had a real crush on Terry.

"Does Mark know?" Jenny had asked.

"Of course not," Debra exclaimed. "And he'd better never find out. Mark seems like a quiet kind of guy, but he can get really jealous."

Leaning against the fence, letting the sun beat down on her face, Jenny remembered the night before and allowed herself a few envious thoughts about Debra.

Everything comes so easily to Debra, she thought.

One boyfriend right after another.

Debra is such a secure person. She's so lucky.

She was still leaning against the fence rail, thinking about Debra, when the solitary rider came into view. He was approaching slowly along the path from the woods, his horse plodding, head down.

Jenny didn't remember saddling up a solitary rider this morning. Gary must have taken care of him, she thought, watching the man slowly move nearer, his feet pushing the stirrups out over the flanks of the black horse he rode.

The stable didn't get many solitary riders, especially in the morning. People usually rode in couples or groups.

Closer, the rider came. Into clear focus now.

Jenny recognized the horse. James.

What a stupid name for a horse, she thought.

Gary's right. The horses at this stable all have weird names.

As the horse drew nearer, Jenny could hear

the steady *clop-clop-clop* of its hooves on the dirt.

Shielding her eyes from the glare of the sun with one hand, she gazed at the rider.

He was a big man, very broad, wearing a red flannel shirt and gray slacks.

He had close-cropped brown hair that picked up the light of the sun. His face was very red.

He pulled up on the reins as the horse stepped up to the fence directly in front of Jenny. Steadying the horse, he stared down at Jenny with cold, steely-gray eyes.

His forehead was beaded with perspiration. His mouth was twisted in a crooked smile.

He leaned forward over the horse's neck.

Jenny stared up at him, her eyes locked on his cold gray eyes.

"Hi. I'm back," he said in a rough, gravelly voice.

Jenny stared wide-eyed into Mr. Hagen's face.

Then she opened her mouth and started to scream.

Chapter 11

The next evening, Debra paced back and forth across her room, holding the cordless phone to her ear as she talked to Mark.

The curtains at the window fluttered and flapped in a stiff breeze. Outside, she could see a tiny patch of blue sky between heavy, dark rainclouds. It had rained hard all day.

"I guess Jenny is okay today," she told Mark, lowering her voice in case her cousin was nearby. "She hasn't come home from the stable yet."

"But what happened to her yesterday?" Mark asked.

Debra stared out the window at the widening patch of blue sky. "She freaked out. Just totally freaked," she replied.

"Huh? What do you mean?" Mark sounded confused.

"She thought she saw that man who died.

Mr. Hagen. I told you the whole story, Mark. Jenny keeps seeing him everywhere."

"You mean she thinks he's still alive?" Mark asked.

"I don't know," Debra said, glancing at the bedroom doorway. "I think Jenny thinks Mr. Hagen is coming back from the grave or something. She's really obsessed."

"Weird," Mark said softly. "So what happened at the stable?"

"Some guy rides up, and Jenny thinks he's Mr. Hagen. So she starts to scream. She screamed so loud, the poor guy nearly fell off his horse. I guess it took them a long time to calm her down."

"Wow," Mark exclaimed. "That's terrible."

"Jenny told me that afterwards she felt like a total jerk. She was so embarrassed. But she really couldn't help herself. She really thought the guy on the horse was Mr. Hagen."

"So then she went back to the stable this morning?" Mark asked.

"Yeah." Debra glanced again at the door. She thought she heard voices in the hall. "Jenny says she likes the job. I just hope she can keep herself together. She — "

Jenny entered the room, greeting Debra with a wave.

"I've got to go, Mark," Debra said into the

phone, smiling at Jenny. "Jenny just got home."

"Okay. Later," Mark replied.

"Hey, I'm baby-sitting at Mrs. Wagner's tonight," Debra added. "Are you going to come by? The usual time?"

"I can't," Mark said after a short pause. "I have to go somewhere with my dad."

Debra uttered a disappointed groan. "Are you sure you can't come?"

Mark said he was sure. They said good-bye.

"So how'd it go today? You get drenched?" Debra asked Jenny, setting the phone down on her dressertop.

"It was okay," Jenny said, picking up a string of brightly colored beads from Debra's dressing table. "We stayed in the stable, mostly. It was kind of boring. No one wants to ride horses in the rain."

"So what'd you do all day? Just feed the horses and clean up and stuff?"

Jenny slipped the beads around her neck and bent to admire herself in the dressing table mirror. "Yeah. And talked to Gary."

Debra's eyes widened with interest. "Gary? Who's Gary?"

"He's one of the wranglers," Jenny replied, adjusting the beads around her neck. "These are pretty. Where'd you get them?"

"Some guy gave them to me," Debra replied. "Don, I think. They're just plastic."

"But they're pretty," Jenny said, slipping them over her head, then examining them between her hands.

"And you felt okay today?" Debra asked sympathetically.

Jenny nodded. "Fine. No problem." She set the beads down on the dressing table, then bent to straighten her dark hair with her hand. "I'm a mess. I should take a shower. You're baby-sitting tonight?"

"Yeah. In a little while. Mrs. Wagner called to make sure I come on time tonight. She has an exam in her course. She was so pumped up about it, she could barely speak."

"Nice to know I'm not the only nervous person in the world," Jenny said dryly.

Debra suddenly had a devilish smile on her face. "I was thinking of giving Terry a little call before I go," she said.

"Poor Terry," Jenny replied, snickering.

"I think he'll be disappointed if he doesn't hear from me," Debra said, picking up the cordless phone. "I think he's starting to really enjoy having a secret admirer."

Jenny sat down on the edge of the bed. "Aren't you afraid he's going to recognize your voice?"

Debra thought about it for a long moment. Then her smile grew wider. "No. Not too afraid."

They both laughed.

"I have to admit, I get pretty turned on by these calls," Debra said. "What does that say about me?"

"That you're totally sick," Jenny replied, teasing.

Debra raised the phone and started to push Terry's number. But she suddenly stopped halfway through it. "Hey, I've got an idea."

"Uh-oh," Jenny replied, rolling her eyes.

Debra held the phone out to her cousin. "You do it."

Jenny's mouth dropped open. "Huh?"

"You make the call," Debra insisted, waving the phone in Jenny's face.

Jenny made no attempt to take it from her. "Me? Why?"

"Because it'll be funny," Debra replied. "And it'll totally mess him up."

"I can't!" Jenny cried.

"Take it. Take it." Debra shoved the phone in Jenny's face.

Jenny had no choice. She took the phone. "I can't. Really, Debra," she pleaded. "What should I say?"

"You'll think of something," Debra said,

grinning. "Just whisper sweet nothings in his ear. It's fun. You'll see. And you'll probably get turned on by it, too."

"Oh, yeah. Big thrill," Jenny said sarcastically. She sighed. "Okay, Deb. What's Terry's number?"

Debra told her the number. Then she sat down beside Jenny as Jenny dialed. "Don't be nervous," Debra instructed.

Jenny frowned. "I'm not nervous. I just think this is stu — " She stopped abruptly. Her voice changed to a sexy whisper. "Hello, Terry?"

"Yeah," Terry sounded immediately suspicious.

"Hi, Terry," Jenny whispered. "You don't know me, but I've been watching you."

Jenny glanced at Debra. Debra covered her mouth with her hand to suppress her giggles.

"Who is this? Is this Debra?" Terry demanded.

"Huh?" Jenny nearly dropped the phone.

"Debra, I know it's you," Terry said triumphantly.

"No, it's not Debra," Jenny uttered in her sexiest whisper. "I don't know anyone named Debra. Let's not talk about other girls, Terry. I just want to talk about you and me."

"Debra, give me a break," Terry muttered. "Don told me it was you."

He hung up.

"Oh. Hey!" Jenny dropped the phone to the bed.

"What happened?" Debra demanded.

"He knows," Jenny told her, frowning.

"Huh?"

"Terry knows it's you. Don told him."

Debra jumped to her feet angrily. "Don did *what?* That disgusting creep!"

Jenny picked up the phone to make sure she had turned it off. "The game's over, Deb."

"I don't *believe* Don! He — he's a filthy snitch," Debra fumed. "What right does he have to spoil some perfectly innocent fun?"

Jenny snickered. "It wasn't exactly innocent, was it?"

Debra glanced at the clock. "I've got to go." She shook her head angrily. "Now I have to run and hide every time I see Terry coming. I'm so embarrassed!"

"I warned you," Jenny replied playfully.

"Terry'll never let me live this down. Never!" Debra fretted, tossing her hair behind her shoulders. "And I'll bet he tells everybody."

She furiously kicked a pair of sneakers out of her way. "People will be laughing at me forever!" she wailed. "For the rest of my life!"

"Don't exaggerate," Jenny said softly. "After ten or twenty years, they'll forget. You'd better hurry, Deb. Mrs. Wagner warned you about being late tonight, remember?"

"Oh. Right." Debra checked her hair in the mirror, smoothed the front of her T-shirt, and hurriedly applied some clear lip gloss to her lips. "Why am I doing this?" she asked herself in the mirror. "Mark isn't coming tonight."

She dropped the lip gloss and started to the door. "What are you doing tonight?" she called back to Jenny.

"Not much," Jenny replied. "I'm going to take a long shower. Then maybe read a book."

"Lucky," Debra said. Then she disappeared out the door.

"Thanks for coming on time," Mrs. Wagner said, greeting Debra at the door. Debra followed her into the living room. "Now where did I put my briefcase?"

"It's right over there. On the chair," Debra told her, pointing.

"Oh. Of course." She scratched her thick, frizzy hair. "I don't know why I'm so nervous about this exam. I really know the material forwards and back. But it *does* count for half my grade."

"I get really nervous before tests, too," Debra said.

"What grade are you going to be in?" Mrs. Wagner asked. Then, without waiting for an answer, she said, "Peter's been a little fussy today. I think he may be teething. So he may wake up tonight."

"I can't imagine Peter being fussy," Debra said.

Mrs. Wagner picked up her briefcase, then put it down. She slapped her forehead. "I almost forgot my notes. I left them on my desk."

She fluttered out of the room, was gone for a few seconds, then returned carrying a sheath of papers in her hand.

"All babies are fussy when they're teething. Even Peter," she said, struggling to stuff the stack of notes into her briefcase. "If he cries really hard and you can't get him to stop, you can rub a little rum on his gums."

"Okay," Debra said. "He'll like that."

A few seconds later, Mrs. Wagner was out the door. Debra stood in the middle of the living room and listened to her car start up, then back down the drive.

Debra suddenly felt uncomfortable. The room, with all its figurines and photos and

knickknacks, seemed smaller and more cluttered than usual. She took a deep breath. The
air was so stuffy.

It was so . . . quiet.

Hope I'm not getting claustrophobic, Debra
thought. Maybe I'd better get out of this living
room.

She made her way silently up the stairs and
tiptoed into Peter's room. He was sleeping on
his stomach, snoring gently. An angel, as
usual.

Feeling a little better, Debra padded down
the stairs.

Why am I so out of sorts tonight? she
wondered.

Is it because Mark isn't coming?

She realized it was the first time she'd been
all alone in Mrs. Wagner's house for an entire
evening.

Maybe that's why the place seemed so much
quieter, so much stuffier, the cluttered living
room so much stranger.

Feeling a sudden tingle of fear, Debra decided to make sure the doors were locked. She
checked the front door, then made her way
quickly back to the kitchen.

To her surprise, the kitchen door was wide
open.

"Weird," she said aloud.

Mrs. Wagner always kept it closed.

She stopped in the center of the room, suddenly filled with fear. Had someone come into the house through the kitchen door?

She turned and glanced quickly around the large kitchen.

No one there.

Debra, stop spooking yourself, she scolded.

She moved quickly to the door, slammed it shut, and turned the lock.

She stared out into the dark backyard for a moment. No one there, either.

You're okay, Debra. There's no one else here, she assured herself. You're just a little edgy tonight. You're probably still upset about Don squealing to Terry that you were his "secret admirer."

Yes, that's it, she decided. I'm still upset about that. That's all.

She removed a can of Coke from the refrigerator, popped the top open, and took a few sips.

I wonder if Mark is still home, she thought, eyeing the wall phone. "Mark will cheer me up," she said aloud. Her voice sounded tiny, almost choked. She cleared her throat and punched Mark's number.

She let the phone ring eight times. No one picked it up.

Disappointed, she replaced the receiver. She needed to talk to someone. It would help kill the time. And it would help her get rid of that uncomfortable feeling that something was wrong tonight, something was strange.

Besides, weren't baby-sitters *supposed* to spend the whole night talking on the phone?

Should I call Jenny? she asked herself.

Should I call Terry?

No. No way. I'll probably never speak to Terry again. I'd be too embarrassed.

I'll call Jenny, she decided.

But just as she reached for the receiver, the phone rang.

"Oh!" she jumped back, startled.

Maybe it's Mark.

She grabbed the receiver. "Hello?"

"Hi, Babes." A low, whispered voice.

"Mark? Is that you? I can't hear you very well."

"It's Mr. Hagen."

"Huh? Who?!" Debra exclaimed.

The voice was dry, like the crackling of dead leaves, and sounded as if it were coming from far away. Debra had to struggle to hear the words. And when she heard them, she felt her entire body go cold with terror:

"I'm alive. I'm back. Company's coming, Babes."

Chapter 12

"Did you tell Jenny about the call?" Mark asked.

Debra shook her head. "No. Of course not. She'd only freak."

Mark leaned forward and kissed her. She felt his arm slip around her shoulders. He pulled her close.

They kissed for a long time.

When it ended, she sat back on the car seat breathlessly and rolled down the window on the passenger side. Cool air filtered into the car. She closed her eyes and smiled. The air felt soothing on her hot face.

They were parked in Mark's blue Civic under the old abandoned railroad trestle near Miller Woods. It was a popular spot for Glenview students to park. But tonight, except for a two-door Buick Skylark on the other end of the long trestle, they were the only ones there.

Debra had described to Mark the frightening, whispered phone call of the night before. He had listened thoughtfully, tapping the steering wheel rhythmically with his thumbs, shaking his head in bewilderment.

"Who could it have been?" he asked. "Who would play such a dumb joke?"

"Jenny would probably say it wasn't a joke," Debra replied, letting the cool breeze flutter through her hair. "She would probably say it was Mr. Hagen, back from the grave."

Mark thought about it for a while. "But if it was Mr. Hagen, why would he call you and not Jenny?"

Debra laughed scornfully. "Because it *wasn't* Mr. Hagen, of course!" she cried. "Because it was someone playing a mean joke on *me!*"

"But — but — I don't get it." Mark tapped his fingers nervously on the steering wheel. "Maybe they made a mistake. Maybe they *thought* they were talking to Jenny."

Debra shook her head. "No way. Why would Jenny be baby-sitting at Mrs. Wagner's?" She rolled down the passenger window all the way. "Whoever was calling *had* to know it was me. Not Jenny."

"So it had to be someone who knows you, right?" Mark said, staring up at the dark, shadowy trestle through the windshield. "And someone who also knows what happened to Jenny back in Harrison."

"Yeah. That's right," Debra agreed softly. She pressed her face against the shoulder of his shirt.

"So who could it be?" Mark asked, slipping his arm around her shoulders again. "Who knows about that guy who tried to kill Jenny — Hagen?"

"Well . . ." Debra thought hard. "You do!"

Mark chuckled. "Yeah. Right. You told me the whole story."

"So it could have been you making the scary call," Debra said. She raised her head and smiled up at him.

He gazed down at her uncertainly. "You're kidding, right?"

She slapped his shoulder gently. "Of *course* I'm kidding. Don't be stupid. Now let's think. Who else knows?" She leaned forward to see his face. "Did you tell anyone?"

"Uh . . . well . . ." Even in the pale moonlight, she could see him blush. He avoided her eyes. "Yeah. I told a couple of guys," he confessed, muttering the words quickly.

"A couple of guys? Why?"

He shrugged, embarrassed. "We were hanging out. At the Dairy Freez. You know. Just talking and stuff. And I thought it was a pretty weird story. So . . ."

"So you told it?"

"Yeah. Sorry, Deb. I didn't know — "

"Who was there?" she demanded. "Who did you tell it to?"

"Well . . . Jon Hart was one," Mark said, shifting uncomfortably in his seat. "And Davey Marcus. That's all. Oh — and Terry, of course. You know. Terry has a summer job at the Dairy Freez. That's why we were there. Because he can sneak us free cones."

Debra gasped. "Terry? Terry Donnelly?"

Mark nodded. "Yeah. You know. Terry." He cast a suspicious glance at her. "What about Terry?"

"Nothing," Debra answered quickly.

I can't tell Mark about my dumb calls to Terry, Debra thought. He'll only get jealous. It takes so little to make Mark jealous.

"Come on. What about Terry?" Mark demanded. "Why did you gasp like that when I said Terry's name?"

"I didn't," Debra lied. "Why are you giving me a hard time? I hardly know Terry."

Mark continued to stare at her, studying her face.

Terry's the one, Debra thought.

It's clear to me now.

I can't tell Mark how I know. But Terry is definitely the one who made the creepy phone call.

He was paying me back for making a fool of him with my silly "secret admirer" calls.

Terry decided to make a secret call of his own. He heard Mark tell Jenny's terrifying story and decided he could use it to scare me.

Well, Terry doesn't know me very well, she thought angrily.

I don't scare so easy.

I'm going to visit Terry tomorrow at his job and let him know that I know what he did. And I'm going to tell him what a total creep I think he is.

"What are you thinking about, Deb?" Mark's voice broke into her angry thoughts.

"Nothing much. Really," she told him.

"You seem so far away," he complained.

"No. I'm right here," she said. She reached up, pulled his face down to hers, and kissed him.

The big blue-and-white sign in front of the Dairy Freez showed a smiling, red-haired boy, Dairy Freez Fred, holding up an enormous triple-scoop vanilla cone, a smear of white ice cream spread across his chin and cheeks.

"How gross," Debra said aloud, pulling her car into the lot and parking in the back. "And why can't they spell 'Freeze' right?"

She pushed open the glass door and angrily strode up to the counter. She saw Terry immediately. He was in back, filling one of the soft ice cream dispensers.

He was concentrating on not spilling the syrup, and didn't see her at first. Debra studied his uniform, frowning in disapproval. He was wearing a Dairy Freez Fred cap and a long white apron, stained with chocolate, also emblazoned with the grinning halfwit, Dairy Freez Fred.

Terry was short and thin. His curly blond hair, which he never seemed to brush, stuck out on all sides of his uniform cap. He looks like a little boy behind that enormous apron, Debra thought.

"Terry — hey!" she leaned over the counter to shout at him.

He looked up, startled to hear his name. Recognizing her, he smiled. "Hi, Debra."

He finished filling the machine, replaced the top, then strolled up to the counter, wiping his hands on a chocolate-stained rag.

"I can't give you any vanilla," he said, his green eyes peering into hers. "I just filled the machine. It takes a while to freeze."

"I don't want vanilla," Debra answered curtly.

"It's weird seeing you in person," he said, not seeming to notice her coldness. "Usually I just hear you whispering on the phone."

Debra could feel herself blushing. "That was just a joke," she sputtered.

"Ha-ha," he said sarcastically. He grinned. "I knew it was you all along."

"Liar," Debra said, frowning. "You did not."

"Sure, I did, Deb. I've always known you were hot for my bod."

"Shut up, Terry," Debra said, rolling her eyes. "I didn't come here to talk about *my* phone calls. I want to talk about *yours*."

"Huh? Mine?" His face filled with surprise.

"Did you call me two nights ago at Mrs. Wagner's house?" Debra demanded, staring at him hard. "Come on. The truth."

It was Terry's turn to blush. "Well . . . uh . . . yeah. I did call you," he confessed.

Chapter 13

"Huh?" Debra gaped at Terry, feeling a surge of anger and surprise. "But — why? I mean — "

"I tried to call you, but you weren't there," Terry said. "I called too late. You'd already left. I got Mrs. Wagner instead."

Debra stared hard at Terry, letting his words sink in. "You mean you weren't the one — ?"

"Mrs. Wagner sounded really nice," Terry said. He suddenly noticed the stunned expression on Debra's face. "Hey, Debra, what's wrong? What did I do?"

"Nothing." She shook her head, trying to clear it. "I — uh — I got a scary call the other night," she explained. "Some creep. I thought it was you."

Terry snickered. "No. It was some other creep."

"I'm sorry," Debra said, backing away from the counter. She saw that the other two white-aproned workers were staring at them. "I'm sorry about the dumb phone calls I made to you." She could feel herself blushing.

"Hey, no problem," Terry muttered, blushing, too. "I kind of enjoyed them." He laughed, a nervous giggle.

He's so cute, Debra thought. Even in that stupid apron and cap.

She wondered if she and Terry would ever go out, ever be a couple. Suddenly, an idea popped into her mind. "You know, my cousin Jenny is staying with me for the summer," she told Terry, leaning over the counter so she could speak softly. "She's really great."

"Oh, yeah?" Terry pretended not to be too interested.

"Maybe the four of us could do something Friday night," she suggested. "You know. Mark and me. And you and Jenny. I think you'd like her."

Terry gazed at her skeptically. "Is this another joke, Debra? Is your cousin eight years old or something?"

"No. Actually she's forty-two," Debra joked.

They both laughed. Debra described Jenny to him. Terry lifted his cap and scratched his hair. His expression suddenly turned serious.

"Oh, wait. Is this the girl Mark was telling me about? The one who was a baby-sitter? The kid's father tried to kill her?"

Debra nodded solemnly. "Yeah. Poor thing. She's had a rough time. But she's really a terrific girl, Terry. I think you'd have a good time."

Terry carefully replaced his cap. He grinned at Debra. "I'll think about it," he said. Then he added dryly, "But with *you* involved, I know there's got to be a catch."

The catch is that I'd rather be going out with you myself, Debra thought, waving good-bye.

Friday night the four of them went to a very silly Chevy Chase movie at the tenplex at the mall. Terry giggled like a hyena throughout the entire movie. Jenny, sitting on the aisle, kept casting glances down the row at Debra, rolling her eyes as if to say, "What's *with* this guy?"

Oh, great, Debra thought unhappily. Jenny *hates* Terry. She's having a terrible time.

But when the movie ended, Jenny and Terry walked up the aisle arm in arm, giggling together.

Watching them, Debra felt a pang of jealousy.

Mark had a cold and kept wiping his nose on a shredded piece of tissue. He was in a sullen mood because of the cold and had barely said three words to Debra the entire night.

Terry, on the other hand, was in a jolly mood. He seemed excited to be with Jenny. As they walked to Mark's car, Terry talked enthusiastically about other Chevy Chase comedies he'd seen, telling some of the funniest parts, making Jenny and Debra both laugh giddily.

I've got to stop thinking about Terry, Debra scolded herself, sliding into the passenger seat next to Mark. I've got to stop being envious of Jenny.

Mark is a great guy. He's just in a crummy mood because of his cold. I like Mark a lot.

So why do I wish I were with Terry?

Why does this always happen to me when I'm going with a guy? Why do I immediately find a guy who seems a lot more fun and interesting?

Mark drove them across town to Page's, a small coffee shop that had bookshelves crammed with books on every wall. Jenny and Terry giggled together in the backseat of the car. Mark kept his eyes straight ahead on the road, sneezing and wiping his nose as he drove.

"Do you feel really lousy?" Debra asked, keeping as far from him as possible so as not to catch his cold. "Do you want to go home?"

"No, I'm fine," Mark insisted. "Really."

Squeezed into a small booth at the restaurant, the four of them talked about school and kids they knew. Jenny told about how she had almost ended up working in a doughnut store for the summer. She had them all laughing when she described her interview for the job and how she had seen the manager gobbling doughnuts the minute she left.

Terry started to tease Debra about the whispered phone calls she had made to him.

Debra caught the shocked expression on Mark's face and cut Terry off immediately. Terry blushed, realizing what he'd done.

"What calls?" Mark asked Terry.

"Uh . . . calls?" Terry asked, playing dumb.

"You just said something about Debra calling you," Mark insisted, turning his gaze on Debra.

"I just called him about Jenny," Debra replied, thinking quickly. "You know. To see if he wanted to go out tonight."

"Yeah. That's right," Terry added quickly, not very convincingly.

But Mark appeared to accept the explanation. He settled back in the booth and sipped his milk shake thoughtfully.

That was a close one, Debra thought, glancing at Jenny. Jenny and Terry were laughing together about something.

Serves me right, Debra thought. I deserve to get caught.

Why did I make those calls to Terry? Even Jenny thought I was weird for doing it.

She sighed to herself.

I guess I have a bigger crush on Terry than I'm willing to admit.

Forcing away those thoughts, she squeezed Mark's arm, then took another few bites of her hamburger.

"Good night, guys," Jenny said, pushing open the back door of the car. "See you, Terry." She flashed him a warm smile, then climbed out.

"I'll call you, Jenny," Terry said, sliding across the seat and climbing out of the car after her. "Sometime this week, okay?"

Debra gave Mark a quick good-night kiss on the cheek. "Feel better," she told him. Then she joined Jenny and Terry in the driveway.

They all said good night again. Debra wondered if Terry was going to kiss Jenny good night.

She found herself feeling relieved when he didn't. He climbed into the passenger seat beside Mark. He slammed the door and waved through the window to Jenny.

Jenny and Debra watched the car back down the drive and pull away. Then they turned and began to make their way to Debra's house.

It was a clear, warm night, sultry for June. A pale, half moon hung just over the sloping rooftop, surrounded by shimmering stars.

"I like Terry," Jenny said happily. "He's funny."

"Yeah. He's great," Debra agreed. "I think he liked you, too. I mean, he said he'd call you and everything."

Their sneakers crunched on the gravel drive. Crickets suddenly started to chirp all around them, a shrill siren.

"Thanks," Jenny said, squeezing Debra's elbow. "Thanks for everything."

Debra started to reply, but stopped.

Following Debra's gaze, Jenny stopped, too, and uttered a low cry of surprise.

Something was lying in the low shrub beside the front stoop.

Something pale and pink.

"What on earth?!" Debra exclaimed. She started to move toward it. But Jenny pulled her back.

"What is it?" Debra whispered.

"An animal," Jenny replied, holding onto her cousin. "No. It's — "

They took a step closer. Then another.

In the pale light, they could see a small, round head. Arms and legs, sprawled over the shrub.

"It — it's not moving," Debra declared. "I think it's — "

"Ohh." Jenny let out a terrified moan. "Debra — it's a baby!"

Chapter 14

Jenny uttered another low moan and sank to her knees on the gravel driveway.

Her eyes locked in horror on the unmoving pink figure. Debra raised her hands to her face and took a step back. Her entire body convulsed in a shudder of terror.

It's Peter, she thought.

"Maybe — it's alive," Jenny choked out.

Taking a deep breath and holding it, Debra ignored her pounding heart and made her way to the front stoop.

It's Peter, she thought. Peter.

I know it's Peter.

How did he get here? Who *put* him here?

She gasped as she came nearer.

And picked it up in one hand.

"Jenny — " she called, her voice trembling. "Look! It's a doll! It's not a baby. It's a doll!" As Debra held up the naked, pink doll, a strange laugh escaped her lips, joy and fear and relief and horror all mixed together.

"Huh?" Jenny climbed unsteadily to her feet. She walked reluctantly toward Debra, as if not quite believing her.

"It's a doll!" Debra declared, laughing the strange laugh again.

"But how — ?" Jenny started. "I mean, who put it there, Deb?" She stepped beside Debra and took the doll from her hands.

And saw the small piece of paper dangling on a ribbon around the doll's neck. "It — it's a note," Jenny stammered, reaching for it with a trembling hand.

Debra grabbed it first and pulled it off the ribbon. She unfolded it and raised it close to read it in the dim light.

"Ohh." She uttered a low gasp as the scrawled words came into focus:

"Hi, Babes. I'm back. See you real soon. Mr. Hagen."

"This can't be happening," Jenny wailed. "It just can't!" She raked her hands back through her dark hair.

Debra shook her head thoughtfully, but didn't reply.

They had made cups of hot chocolate to calm themselves and carried them up to Debra's room. Jenny had kicked off her sneakers and dropped onto the edge of the bed. Debra slumped into the desk chair. She held the doll in her lap, rolling it over in her hands.

"Put it down. Please," Jenny pleaded. "I really can't stand to look at it." She shuddered.

"Take it easy, Jen," Debra said with concern. "It was just a dumb joke, after all."

"It's *not* a joke," Jenny insisted shrilly.

Debra obediently lowered the doll to the floor, pushing it under her chair, out of sight. She took a sip of hot chocolate, cradling the white mug in her lap.

"He's back," Jenny said, her voice a whisper. "This time, he's really back."

Debra stared intently at her cousin. "You don't really believe that, do you?"

Jenny, lost in thought, didn't reply.

"Jenny, listen to me," Debra pleaded. "Jenny?"

Jenny still didn't reply.

Debra stood up and, carrying her mug of hot chocolate, crossed the room and sat down beside Jenny on the edge of the bed. "Jenny?"

Jenny finally looked up. Debra saw that she had chewed her lower lip so hard, it was bleeding.

"He's back," Jenny whispered. "He's alive."

Debra shook her head. "It's a dumb joke, Jen. A really cruel, dumb joke."

"But who — ?" Jenny started. "Who would *do* this to me?"

Debra sighed. She took another sip of hot chocolate. It was too hot and burned her tongue, but it was helping to calm her. "I'm not sure it *was* for you," she told Jenny softly.

"Huh?" Jenny reacted with surprise.

"Someone might be doing this to *me*," Debra told her.

"I — I don't understand." Jenny slid back in the bed and rested her head against the headboard.

"I didn't want to tell you about this, but I guess I have to now," Debra said reluctantly. "Someone called me the other night. At Mrs. Wagner's. Someone whispering. A hoarse kind of whisper. He said he was Mr. Hagen. He said he was alive. He said — "

"I *knew* it!" Jenny cried, her face turning pale. "I knew he was alive. I knew he'd come back to — "

"Jenny, stop!" Debra reached out with both hands and grabbed Jenny's trembling shoulders. "Please. Listen to me."

"But why did Mr. Hagen call *you*?" Jenny demanded, lost once again in her own thoughts.

"Because it wasn't Mr. Hagen," Debra insisted, holding on firmly to her cousin's shoulders, trying desperately to get through to her. "It's some stupid creep, playing a stupid joke. It *has* to be. People don't come back from the dead."

Jenny locked her eyes on Debra's. "Don't they?" Her words were more a challenge than a question. "Don't they, Debra?"

"No," Debra insisted, releasing Jenny's shoulders and climbing to her feet. "Let's think. Let's think of who could be doing this. Who made the call? Who left the doll in the shrub with the note?"

"I don't know," Jenny said weakly, biting her bleeding lip.

Debra began to pace back and forth, holding the hot chocolate mug between her hands. "I have a confession to make," she said after a while, avoiding Jenny's eyes. "I hope you won't be mad."

"Confession?" Jenny seemed to be only half-listening.

"I told Mark about you. About what happened to you back in Harrison. The whole story."

"That's okay," Jenny replied softly.

Debra continued to avoid Jenny's gaze.

"Well, Mark told a few other kids. Terry and a couple of other guys."

Jenny didn't reply.

"But I really don't think Mark or Terry or the others would do anything like this," Debra said, thinking out loud. "I really don't."

"That's because it really is Mr. Hagen," Jenny said with a shiver.

"No," Debra insisted. "No way."

"I just don't understand why he called *you*," Jenny repeated, ignoring her cousin.

The curtains fluttered at the window. A gust of hot, wet air blew into the room.

"Let's think," Debra said, starting to pace again. "Who could it be? Who?" She stopped in the middle of her bedroom and turned to Jenny. "I just had a flash."

Jenny shifted her weight on the bed. "What?"

"Did someone follow you up here?" Debra asked, her eyes lighting up excitedly.

"Huh?"

"Did someone follow you? Did you give my address to anyone?" Debra demanded.

Jenny stared back at her, thinking hard. "Just Cal," she replied finally. "But he — "

"Cal?" Debra dropped down onto the bed at Jenny's feet.

"You know. My boyfriend back home,"
Jenny told her. "But Cal wouldn't do anything
like that."

"Does he know the whole story?" Debra
asked.

Jenny nodded. "Yes. He knows everything.
But I'm telling you, Deb, he would never play
a mean joke like this. He knows me too well.
He knows how upset it would make me . . ."
Her voice trailed off.

"You gave him my address?" Debra asked.
"My phone number?"

"Yeah," Jenny said. "But Cal isn't up here.
He was going to get a summer job back in Harrison. He was going to — "

"Call him," Debra demanded. She jumped
up and hurried to the desk to get the cordless
phone.

"Huh?" Jenny pulled herself to a sitting
position.

"Call him right now," Debra insisted excitedly. "Let's prove that it isn't him. Let's cross
him off the list." She pushed the phone into
Jenny's lap.

"But, Deb — "

"Call him," Debra ordered, pointing to the
phone. "We might just solve the mystery right
now."

"No. It isn't Cal," Jenny said softly. But she

obediently picked up the phone and punched Cal's number.

The phone rang once. Twice.

"It isn't Cal. You'll see," Jenny said confidently, holding the phone tightly against her ear, listening to the steady, rhythmic ringing. "You'll see."

Chapter 15

Cal's mother answered after the fourth ring. Her voice sounded hoarse, as if she'd been sleeping.

"Hi, Mrs. Barton," Jenny said nervously. "It's me. Jenny. Did I wake you?"

"Yeah. I guess," came the gruff reply.

"Oh. Sorry. I didn't realize how late it is. Can I speak to Cal?"

"No," Mrs. Barton said.

"Huh? Is he home?" Jenny asked, startled by the curt reply.

Cal's mother cleared her throat noisily. "He isn't here, Jenny," she said finally.

"You mean he's out on a date or something?" Jenny asked, puzzled.

"He ran away," Mrs. Barton said. "Last week. We had one of our fights. About the car. And you know how impulsive Cal can be."

"Yes, I know — " Jenny started.

"Well, he ran away and we haven't seen him for a week. His father and I are worried sick about him." She coughed. Then she asked anxiously, "Is Cal up there? Did he follow you up there?"

"Uh . . . I'm not sure. . . ." Jenny replied.

White sunlight poured down on the stable, capturing everything in its hot glow. The ground sparkled up at the shimmering silver sky. The horses bobbed their heads nervously, expectantly, shifting their weight, tossing their tails, seemingly eager to get moving.

Jenny saddled a tall palomino, standing in the shade made by the horse. The heat seemed to radiate up from the hard ground. The sun is draining all my energy, she thought, struggling to pull the straps tight.

I feel so heavy, even out of the sun.

So heavy and tired.

The horse tossed its head, the pale yellow mane glistening under the brilliant sunlight.

Jenny raised a hand to shield her eyes from the sun. She tugged at the reins, but the horse resisted.

She tugged harder.

Someone was waiting for the horse, waiting in the deep shadow by the side of the stable.

"Come on, girl!" Jenny tugged the reluctant horse away from the fence.

Sunlight danced off the tall grass that fringed the narrow path.

"Come on, girl. Someone's waiting. I know it's hot, but it's time to go to work."

The horse uttered a low whinny and followed her slowly toward the stable, its hooves thudding loudly on the hard ground.

A flock of dark birds swooped overhead, black V's against the white-silver sky.

Jenny felt the heat of the sun on her shoulders and the back of her neck. It's weighing me down, she thought.

I feel heavier than this horse.

"Come on, girl."

As the horse neared the stable, the waiting figure stepped out from the shadows. Moving quickly, he raised his sneakered foot to the stirrup and hoisted himself silently into the saddle.

The sun glowed brighter. Brighter still.

Jenny shielded her eyes with both hands.

The horse whinnied. The rider found the other stirrup, then righted himself, adjusting his weight on the horse's straight back.

"All set?" Jenny asked. "Feel comfortable?"

The rider didn't answer.

The ground shimmered white. Heat rose up from the dirt.

"Everything okay?" Jenny asked.

Still no reply.

She raised her eyes to the rider.

"Cal!" she cried.

He grinned down at her, his spiky blond hair gleaming like white fire in the blinding sunlight.

"Cal! What are you *doing* here?" Jenny demanded happily.

He didn't reply. Instead he leaned toward her and stretched out his hands.

"Cal — no!"

But he grabbed her hands and tugged hard.

"Cal — please!"

With surprising strength, he lifted her up onto the saddle in front of him.

"Cal, what are you *doing?*"

He took up the reins and the horse bolted forward. The sudden burst pushed Jenny back. She leaned against Cal, his arms around her, the reins tight in one hand.

The horse bounced beneath her. She could hear the hard thud of hooves on the trail.

"Cal — I have a job to do," Jenny cried. "I can't come with you. Cal?"

His arms felt so good around her shoulders. She leaned against his chest, feeling secure.

The trail led up to sloping hills, brown from the summer sun. Tall pines jutted up on both sides of them, whirring past in a blur, glistening golden in the white light.

"Cal — we have to go back!" Jenny cried, shouting over the steady *clop clop* of the big palomino's hooves.

She didn't want to go back. She wanted to stay secure in his arms, wrapped up by him, and ride forever through the trees.

The hot wind blew against her face, ruffled her dark hair behind her.

And then, suddenly, Cal pulled back hard on the reins.

Jenny felt the horse's body tense. She watched its head pull up.

Cal tugged harder.

The horse stopped abruptly, silently. The hot air swirled around Jenny.

"Cal, we can't stop here. We have to go back."

Leaning snugly against him, Jenny turned and smiled up at him.

The sun beamed down, blinding her at first.

But Cal's face slowly came into focus.

His dark eyes burned into hers, as hot as the sun. And as she stared, the dark pupils faded — until he stared back at her with eggshell-white eyes. Solid white.

No pupils. No pupils at all. The blank stare of the dead.

He grinned. And as he grinned, his skin began to peel away, chunks of pink skin sliding down like Silly Putty, then dropping onto his shoulders, falling to the ground — until Jenny stared in horror at a grinning, gray-boned skeleton.

"Nooooo!" Her scream echoed off the dry, brown hills.

His white eyes stared blankly at her.

"Let go!" She frantically struggled to pull away.

But his powerful arms circled around her. And as they tightened around her waist, she realized the flesh had fallen away from his arms, too.

He was only bone now.

A skeleton with the inhuman strength of the dead.

The bones encircled her, tightened around her, holding her, pressing her tight against the leering skeleton.

"At last I've got you, Jenny!" its voice, dry as the swirling dust on the path, cried triumphantly.

"At last I am going to take you to the grave with me!"

"No, Mr. Hagen!" Jenny shrieked, still struggling to free herself from the skeletal grip. "Mr. Hagen — please! Let me go!"

Chapter 16

Debra glanced at the clock in the center of the cluttered mantelpiece. Eight thirty-five. "Mark, where are you?" she said aloud.

She started to pace back and forth, her arms crossed over her chest. But Mrs. Wagner's living room was too small and crowded for pacing. Debra stopped, afraid she might bump a table or shelf.

It was Monday night. Mrs. Wagner had hurried off to her class at the community college, late as usual. Debra was looking forward to seeing Mark.

The floors creaked under the worn carpet. Debra sat down on the arm of the couch.

Why am I so jumpy tonight? she wondered. Every sound startles me.

I wish Mark would hurry up and get here. I could really use some company tonight.

A scrabbling sound above her head made her

gasp. She gripped the couch arm and listened.

Probably a squirrel running across the roof.

That's all. Just a squirrel, she assured herself, forcing her heartbeat to slow to normal.

I'm getting as nervous as Jenny, she thought unhappily.

Was that Mark's car on the street?

She hurried to the living room window and pushed aside the curtains to see out.

No. Just a car passing.

She pulled the curtains back into place.

Poor Jenny, she thought. She's been having the worst nightmares ever since Friday night. Dreams about her boyfriend Cal and Mr. Hagen, the two of them all mixed together.

Yuck, Debra thought, tossing her blonde hair behind her shoulders.

Poor kid. She's really messed up over this Mr. Hagen thing.

She's just so terrified. She really thinks that horrible man is going to come back from the grave to get her.

I'd better call her later and see how she's doing.

Again Debra heard the scrabbling sound, like someone climbing around upstairs.

I'm kind of freaked about everything, too, she admitted to herself.

I mean, I'm the one who got the call last week.

What if some nut is after Jenny — and me, too?

No. Stop. Stop it right now, she scolded herself.

I'm not going to get all frightened because someone is playing a dumb joke.

But what *is* that sound upstairs?

Walking with determined strides, she crossed the living room to the stairs and hurried up to investigate. Stopping at the landing, she peered down the long hall. It was empty and dark.

Taking a deep breath, she stepped into Peter's room and crept up to the side of the crib. The baby was sleeping fitfully, breathing in short gasps and thrashing his slender arms as if having a bad dream.

He looked so distressed, Debra was tempted to pick him up and soothe him. But she decided not to wake him. She checked to make sure he was dry, then tiptoed from the room.

Poor little guy, she thought, heading back downstairs. Is *everyone* having nightmares around here?

The clock on the mantel showed that it was nearly nine.

I'll give Mark a nightmare if he doesn't hurry

up and get here! Debra thought impatiently.

She peered out the living room window. The street was dark and empty.

Maybe Mark's cold got worse and he isn't coming, she thought. She decided to call his house. Taking one last glance out to the street, she turned and headed to the kitchen to use the phone.

Mark answered after the second ring. "Mark — you're home!" Debra exclaimed.

"Yeah," he replied.

"But I don't understand," Debra said. "It's Monday night and — "

"I'm not coming, Debra," Mark interrupted, his voice cold and hard. "Why don't you call Terry to come over there?"

"What?" Debra didn't understand. Why did Mark sound so angry?

"I heard about your little whispered phone calls to Terry," Mark explained.

"You did? Who — ?" Debra started, but stopped herself. "But, Mark — "

" 'Bye, Debra," Mark said coldly.

"Mark, those calls — they were just a joke," Debra said, her voice trembling.

"Everything's a joke," Mark said bitterly. " 'Bye."

He hung up.

"Oh, great!" Debra exclaimed aloud, staring

at the humming phone. "Mark — you're a jealous idiot!"

She slammed the phone down onto the wall and stormed around the room. "Ow!" Her knee bumped a kitchen stool.

"Aaaaagh!" Bending to rub her knee, Debra let out an angry, disgusted cry.

She cut it short, remembering the baby, and listened. She hadn't awakened him.

Who told Mark about the stupid phone calls? She wondered angrily. Was it Terry? Who else knew about them? No one.

Now she'd have to cry and grovel and beg Mark's forgiveness, and make a total fool of herself to get him back.

If she wanted him back.

She leaned her back against the kitchen counter and stared at the wall phone.

Yes. I want him back, she decided.

I don't want him to be angry at me.

She decided to call him right back and apologize. If she made up with him immediately, there might still be time for him to come over tonight.

As she reached for the phone, it rang.

"Oh!" Debra jumped back, startled.

It's Mark, she decided. He feels as bad as I do. He's sorry he was so awful to me. He realizes he was being stupid.

She let it ring a second time.

Should I accept his apology right away?

Yes.

She lifted the receiver to her ear. "Hi, Mark," she said, "I — "

"*Company's coming, Babes,*" a harsh voice whispered menacingly in her ear.

Debra was so startled, she nearly dropped the receiver.

"Who *is* this?" she demanded angrily.

Was it Mark? Was it Mark playing this awful joke on her? The thought stabbed her, stuck like a dark wound in her mind as she listened to the raspy whisper on the other end of the line:

"*It's Mr. Hagen, Debra. I'm alive. And I'm coming for you. Real soon.*"

The voice was so dry, so far away. As if it really were coming from somewhere beyond the grave.

"Who *is* this?" Debra repeated. Her knees suddenly felt weak, about to collapse. She grabbed the countertop with her free hand to support herself. "Mark — if this is you — "

"*I'll be there,*" the voice rasped. "*Wait for me, Debra. Wait for me. I've come from so far away to get you.*"

"NOOOO!" Debra shrieked.

She tried to slam the receiver back on its

holder, but missed. It fell from her hands, swinging wildly back and forth along the wall.

The whispered, raspy voice still echoing in her ears, she ran from the kitchen. Through the hall. Into the brightness of the cluttered living room.

She was in the living room doorway when the howling started.

High-pitched animal howling.

An inhuman wail, like the agonized cry of the living dead.

As she froze in fear, the inhuman howl grew louder.

It's so nearby, she realized, raising her trembling hands to her ears.

The hideous howl rose and fell like a ghoulish siren, a terrifying signal, a call from beyond the grave.

"It — it's inside the house," Debra said aloud.

Chapter 17

Her heart pounding, the howls piercing through the room, Debra held onto the doorframe to steady herself.

It's here. In the house, she realized, gripped with fear.

It — it's upstairs.

She realized she was holding her breath. She let it out slowly and gasped in another one.

As another wail rang out, she suddenly recognized the sound.

It was Peter. Crying.

"He's never cried before," she said out loud. "No *wonder* I didn't recognize the sound!"

Still shaky, but starting to feel the fear drain from her, Debra hurried up the stairs. She found the baby on his back, his face knotted in anger as he cried, thrashing his arms and legs wildly.

"Peter, it's okay. It's okay. I'm here," she said softly, and lifted him carefully from the crib. "It's okay. It's okay."

He stopped crying the instant she picked him up. Opening his dark eyes, he stared up at her and whimpered softly, his face still red from his noisy protests.

"You scared me, fella," Debra said softly, rubbing the crown of his warm head gently till he stopped whimpering. "You really freaked me, you know?"

Peter stared up at her, silent now, his breathing normal.

"I thought you were that dead man, come to get me," Debra said, her voice a gentle whisper. She walked back and forth, holding the baby against her chest, soothing him. He felt so nice, so warm, he was helping to soothe her, too.

"You've got good pipes, Peter," she whispered. "You made quite a sound, fella."

He was drifting back to sleep. She continued walking back and forth, holding him close to her, whispering softly to him.

"First that awful phone call. Then your howls and yowls," she whispered. "You can't blame me for freaking, can you, Peter?"

He was sound asleep, gurgling softly, as she set him back down in his crib. She stood watching him for a few moments, feeling better, feeling calm, watching how peacefully he was sleeping.

But as she made her way back down the stairs, the ugly rasping of the voice over the phone returned to her.

Again she heard the ugly threats.

"Company's coming, Babes."

The ugly, menacing words repeated in Debra's ears, chasing away the feeling of calm she had felt upstairs in Peter's room.

And she remembered something else. She remembered something that tightened her throat and made her feel cold all over.

He had called her by name.

Mr. Hagen — or whoever it was — had called her Debra.

"I've come from so far away to get you, Debra."

He wasn't coming after Jenny. He was coming after her.

"Company's coming, Babes. I'll be there real soon."

But why?

Her head spinning with ugly, frightening thoughts, Debra took a few steps into the living room.

But she stopped short when she heard the scrape of heavy footsteps in the back hall.

Chapter 18

Debra felt a cold shiver travel down her body. She took a hesitant step into the hallway.

"Mark, is that you?"

Had Mark changed his mind? Had he come to Mrs. Wagner's to apologize?

No.

Mark wouldn't come in through the back door. He wouldn't come in without knocking or ringing the bell.

"Who — who's there?" Debra called. Her frightened words came out in a choked whisper.

Mr. Hagen?

The dry, raspy voice on the phone had threatened to come for her. Soon.

"Who's there?" Debra called, a little louder.

No reply.

"Mrs. Wagner?" Debra's quivering voice revealed her fear.

Still no reply.

Then, another scraping footstep. A cough.

Keeping her back pressed against the wall, Debra inched her way to the kitchen. Over the rapid pounding of her heart, she could hear the raspy voice repeating its cold threats in her ear.

"Company's coming, Babes. I'm alive and I'm coming for you."

She stopped just outside the kitchen doorway, her legs trembling. "Mrs. Wagner? Are you home?"

Silence.

A rectangle of yellow light shone into the hallway from the kitchen. Suddenly, as Debra stared in terror, a large shadow moved into the light.

Swallowing hard, her throat as dry as cotton, Debra took a step into the kitchen. "Maggie!" she cried.

The large woman, wearing a bright fuchsia housedress over black leggings, had her back to Debra. She was leaning into a pantry cupboard, moving food cans around.

She turned slowly at the sound of Debra's voice, holding onto the wall with one hand for support.

"Maggie — what are you doing here?"

Debra demanded shrilly, her heart still pounding hard.

Maggie pushed herself away from the cupboard and took a few unsteady, shuffling steps toward Debra, a look of annoyance on her bright red face.

She's been drinking, Debra realized. She's drunk.

"Who are you?" Maggie asked, squinting one eye at Debra.

"I — I'm the baby-sitter," Debra stammered, keeping her distance.

"No. *I'm* the baby-sitter," Maggie insisted, slurring the words together, squinting angrily across the room at Debra. "I'm the baby-sitter."

"Maggie, what do you want?" Debra asked sternly.

"I on'y came for what's mine," the woman replied, tottering to one side.

Debra gasped, afraid Maggie was going to fall over. But the woman caught herself and straightened up, blinking hard as if trying to see Debra clearly.

"You have to leave," Debra insisted, trying to keep her voice steady. "Mrs. Wagner isn't here."

"I on'y came for what is owed me," Maggie repeated. "I'm the baby-sitter, see."

"You'll have to come back when Mrs. Wagner is here," Debra told her. Taking long, hurried strides, she made her way past the tottering woman and pulled open the back door. "Good night, Maggie. You have to leave now."

"I have a key," Maggie said, turning slowly. "I'm the baby-sitter." She took a shuffling step toward the door.

"Good night," Debra said, holding the screen door open for her.

"I'll come back." Maggie stopped a few inches in front of Debra, forcing Debra to step back. Maggie was breathing hard through her open mouth. Her breath smelled sour from a cheap wine.

"Good night," Debra repeated.

Please, please, go away! she pleaded silently.

"I'll come back," Maggie said, teetering toward the door. "I'll come back for what's mine."

Then she made her way slowly out the door.

Debra immediately closed the kitchen door, turning the lock. She stood with her back pressed against the wall, waiting for her heartbeat to slow.

"What a creepy woman!" she declared out loud. "Why does she keep coming here? Just to frighten me?"

The baby started to cry again. Debra hurried upstairs to take care of him.

What a night, she thought unhappily.

A short while later, Mrs. Wagner returned. Debra decided to tell her about Maggie's visit. "She was terribly drunk," Debra said, concluding her story. "She left when I asked her to. But she said she'd come back. This was her second visit. I didn't tell you about the first time."

Mrs. Wagner listened to Debra's story in open-mouthed disbelief. "I told Maggie *never* to come back," she said, shaking her head. "I had to fire her. She was a thief, and she drank all the time. She loved Peter. But I couldn't trust her around him. She was just too irresponsible."

"Well, she still has a key," Debra said. "She scared me to death. When I heard someone in the kitchen, I thought . . ." Her voice trailed off.

"I'll have the locks changed tomorrow," Mrs. Wagner said, frowning. She raised her eyes to Debra. "I don't think Maggie's dangerous, but I don't know for sure. I heard that she had to move out of her house."

"She's homeless?" Debra asked.

Mrs. Wagner nodded. "Yes. That's what I heard. She's living on the streets. Poor woman." She *tsk-tsked*, then kicked her sandals off and rubbed her feet. "It's getting late. I'll see you Wednesday night. I hope Maggie didn't frighten you too much."

"No. I was okay," Debra lied.

An hour later, Debra was lying in bed, staring up at the shifting shadows on her bedroom ceiling, unable to fall asleep. She had been thinking angry thoughts about Mark. He wasn't there when I needed him, she thought. He let me down.

But then she realized that she had let him down, too.

Maybe I'll call Mark tomorrow, she thought. Maybe I'll apologize for those dumb calls to Terry.

Or should I wait for Mark to call me? After all, the calls were just a joke.

She thought about Terry, how cute he looked in his Dairy Freez outfit.

Maybe the calls weren't a joke, Debra told herself.

I'll never get to sleep if I don't stop thinking about all this.

But she couldn't turn off her mind, couldn't stop the swirling images of all that had happened tonight.

Turning onto her side, she found herself

thinking about Maggie. Poor, drunk Maggie, squinting at her under the bright kitchen lights.

Debra wondered what it would be like not to have a home, not to have a place to sleep in, to have to wander from place to place.

Her thoughts turned to Mr. Hagen, to the frightening, whispered phone call.

She was hearing his dry, throaty voice for the hundredth time, replaying his ugly threats in her mind — when she heard the shrill scream of terror.

Debra pulled herself up.

The scream was coming from the next room.

Jenny!

Chapter 19

"Jenny — what happened? Are you okay?" Debra clicked on the light as she burst into Jenny's room.

Jenny sat up groggily in bed and blinked at Debra.

"Jenny — what *is* it?" Debra demanded, her panic revealed in her trembling voice.

"Another nightmare," Jenny said, her throat still clogged with sleep.

Debra let out a long sigh of relief. Then she rushed forward to give her cousin a comforting hug. "Was it the same nightmare?" she asked softly.

Jenny nodded.

"Such a horrible scream," Debra said with a shudder. "I thought — "

"It's a horrible nightmare," Jenny interrupted. "This time, Cal and I were in the car, driving somewhere at night. And Cal's face

changed. His skin dropped off in sickening
chunks. And beneath his face was Mr. Hagen's.
And — "

"What's wrong? What's happening?" Debra's
father demanded. Debra's parents burst into
the room in their nightshirts, their expressions
frightened. "We heard a shriek."

"Jenny had another nightmare," Debra told
them.

"I — I'm sorry," Jenny said, embarrassed.
"I can't help it. I — "

Mrs. Jeffers *tsk-tsk*ed. "You gave us a
scare," Debra's father said, shaking his head.

"I'm okay. Really," Jenny assured them.

"Do you want some hot chocolate?" Mrs. Jeffers asked, squeezing Jenny's hand. "A cup of
tea, maybe? Or something cold? I could run
downstairs and get you something."

"No. Please. I'm fine now," Jenny insisted.

After her parents had gone back to their
room, Debra sat down on the edge of Jenny's
bed. "Speaking of nightmares," she began reluctantly, "I got another phone call tonight. At
Mrs. Wagner's."

Jenny's eyes grew wide with fear. Her fingers tightened around the edge of her blanket.
"From Mr. Hagen?"

"From someone *pretending* to be Mr.
Hagen," Debra corrected her.

"No!" Jenny cried heatedly. "It *is* him. It's him! I know it!"

"Jenny, calm down — *please!*" Debra exclaimed, jumping to her feet. "It isn't Mr. Hagen. It *can't* be. It's someone playing a really cruel joke. Mr. Hagen is dead. He's dead!"

Jenny raised her eyes to Debra, her face pale with fear. "Debra," she said in a whisper, "how do you know for sure?"

The stable was busy the next afternoon. Jenny found it hard to concentrate. She kept thinking about Cal, wondering where he was, wondering if he planned to follow her upstate.

Two day camps arrived at the same time with noisy, excited kids, eager to get up on horses.

Heavy, dark clouds rolled over the sun, casting the stable grounds in an eerie, yellow-gray light. The gusting wind carried drops of rain, an omen of the approaching storm.

Are you coming here, Cal? Jenny wondered, as she tightened the saddle of a patient brown mare. Are you coming to see me?

"Is it ready? Can I climb up?" a redheaded boy in a faded Simpsons T-shirt asked, stirring Jenny from her thoughts.

"Yeah. You're all set," Jenny told him. The

boy lifted his foot into the stirrup. Jenny gave him a boost onto the saddle.

She handed the reins to him and started to guide the horse toward his camp companions. He held the reins uncertainly in one hand, holding onto the saddle horn for dear life with his other hand.

He called something down to Jenny, but she was thinking about her nightmare of the night before, Cal once again turning into Mr. Hagen, and didn't hear him.

Where *are* you, Cal? The question kept repeating in her mind.

"*Hey!*" An angry cry broke into her thoughts. Jenny gazed around the crowded stable.

"Jenny — whoa!"

It took her a while to realize that Gary was calling to her. He was standing beside the red-headed boy on the brown mare, glaring at her angrily.

Seeing his angry expression, Jenny jogged over to him. "Gary, what's wrong?"

"Look." He made a disgusted face and pointed to the right stirrup. Jenny saw immediately that it hung down too far.

"How's this boy supposed to get his foot in the stirrup?" Gary demanded.

"Sorry," Jenny muttered. "I meant to tighten it."

"You sent him off with only one foot in the stirrup," Gary said, turning away from her to tighten it. "He could've fallen. What were you thinking of, Jenny?"

"Uh . . . nothing," Jenny replied, feeling her face grow red.

"There you go, guy," Gary told the boy, fitting his sneakered foot into the stirrup. "How does that feel?"

"Good," the boy said, still holding tightly to the saddle horn.

"Push hard with both feet," Gary said, examining the rest of the saddle straps. After making sure everything was secure, he led the boy over to his group.

Jenny headed to the barn to lead out another horse. She was halfway there when she realized she was being followed. "Oh. Gary. Sorry about that," she said.

He put a hand on her shoulder. "You okay?"

She nodded. "I just wasn't thinking."

"I didn't mean to yell," he said, studying her face. "It's just that . . . well, that was a pretty serious mistake."

"I know." Jenny could feel herself blushing again. She had a sudden urge to tell Gary everything — to tell him she'd been having these horrible nightmares about a dead man who was coming for her.

But instead she said, "I'll concentrate harder. I'm a little out of it today, I guess."

He nodded sympathetically, his eyes locked on hers. "Well, you're all finished for now. Everyone's saddled up. I'm going to lead them out on the trail. Why don't you take a short break?"

"Thanks," she replied gratefully. "And I'm really sorry. About messing up."

He turned and made his way quickly to his horse. She watched him lift himself into the saddle, and trot over to the waiting riders.

Then she raised her eyes to the sky. The dark storm clouds hung low over the hills, moving quickly like a gray-black blanket being pulled over the sky. From somewhere far in the distance, Jenny could hear the insistent rumble of thunder.

I hope Gary gets them all back before the rain starts, she thought.

A horse whinnied shrilly behind her.

"It's okay. It's just thunder," she told it.

Her nightmare flashed through her mind again. Had it been raining in the dream?

She shook her head as if trying to shake the dream from her thoughts. She strode over to the nervous, black stallion and stroked its mane.

She thought of Cal.

Don't think about Cal, she scolded herself.

The horse nodded its head, as if agreeing with her.

Thunderclap. That was the stallion's name.

Stroking the animal's neck, thinking about its name, Jenny had a sudden impulse.

Thunderclap was saddled.

What if I climb on and ride off? Jenny thought.

Gary told me to take a break. Clear my mind.

What if I ride off, gallop away? Into the storm.

Thunderclap is a perfect name for a horse to ride through the rain.

Jenny untethered the tall stallion from the fence railing. She realized her heart had begun to pound. She felt a surge of excitement as she lifted herself into the saddle.

Uttering a low whinny, Thunderclap backed away from the fence, eager to get moving.

Jenny adjusted her weight in the saddle, tightening the reins in her hands.

I used to be a good rider, she thought.

I used to go riding at the Harrison stables often.

But then I stopped.

I stopped doing everything I loved to do.

Well . . . today I'm going to *ride*.

"We're going to ride faster than the rain, aren't we, Thunderclap?" she called down excitedly to the horse. "Between the raindrops!" she exclaimed. "Through the thunder!".

She guided the horse toward the trail, bouncing unsteadily in the saddle, still getting used to the big horse's stride.

The horse began to trot as Jenny followed the trail toward the hills. As the trail narrowed and curved up through the tall pine woods, Jenny quickened the pace to a steady gallop.

It was dark as night in the woods. The wind whipped against her, heavy and wet.

It feels so good, Jenny thought happily. The cold, wet wind. The heavy, rhythmic bounce of the horse. The dark blur of trees whirring by.

The rain came, at first a gentle tapping against the hard ground. And then a steady drumroll. She felt it first in her hair, then on the shoulders of her T-shirt.

Jenny closed her eyes and allowed the horse to carry her, following the curving trail at a gallop.

The rain feels so good . . . so good, she thought.

So peaceful — so *cleansing*.

And then she heard the hoofbeats behind her.

At first she thought she was hearing thunder.

She opened her eyes and listened, not slowing her horse.

The rain pattered loudly against tree leaves.

The woods grew even darker.

The rumble drew closer. Not thunder.

Another horse.

Another horse on the trail, galloping hard.

Jenny gripped the reins tightly. She pushed her sneakered feet hard against the stirrups.

"Ride, Thunderclap! Faster!"

She listened as she rode, the dark woods alive with sound, cracks of thunder, the steady patter of the rain.

And the galloping horse behind her, coming closer.

Closer.

I know who it is, Jenny thought with surprising calm.

I know it's Mr. Hagen.

Riding hard.

I know it's Mr. Hagen.

Coming to collect me.

Chapter 20

Debra peered out the kitchen window at the rain. A bright white flash of lightning illuminated the puddled backyard. In the split second of brightness, Debra saw water sliding off the sloping garage roof, cascading to the ground like a waterfall.

As a roar of thunder followed the lightning, she took a step back from the window. She listened carefully, hoping the loud noise didn't wake up the baby.

When is it going to stop? she wondered. It's been raining hard since the afternoon.

She walked to the wall phone. Leaning against the counter, she picked up the receiver and called home. Her mother answered after the first ring.

"Oh, hi, Mom. It's me."

"Is everything okay?" her mother demanded. "Is the baby okay?"

Why did she always assume that something terrible had happened?

"Yes, Mom. Everything's fine."

"Was the street flooded?" Her mother never ran out of questions. "I heard on the news that the Jefferson Bridge is closed because of the rain."

"I don't go that way," Debra replied, allowing a little impatience to creep into her voice.

"Well, if this rain keeps up . . ." Mrs. Jeffers' voice trailed off.

"I called to talk with Jenny," Debra said, sliding a tall kitchen stool closer and climbing onto it. "Is she home yet?"

"No. Not yet." Mrs. Jeffers couldn't hide the worry in her voice.

"Weird," Debra said. "She should've been home hours ago. Where could she be in this storm?"

"Beats me," her mother replied. "Maybe she went somewhere after work with some friends or something."

"Friends?" Debra asked.

"Well, she mentioned she was getting friendly with the head wrangler there at the stable," Mrs. Jeffers said. Static cut through the line, making her voice sound far away. "Gary somebody, I think."

"But Jenny would phone if she was going to

go out," Debra said shrilly. She decided there was no point in worrying her mother. She quickly softened her tone and added, "I'm sure she's okay. Maybe she's waiting out the storm in the stable."

"Yes. Maybe," her mother replied. "I'll tell her to call as soon as she gets in, Deb."

Debra said good-bye and hung up the receiver. She slid off the tall stool and walked back to the window.

Another flash of lightning. The backyard was lit up, brighter than day. The wet grass glistened eerily, as if electrified.

And what was *that?*

Something moving behind the low cluster of rose bushes?

No. Debra stared into the darkness as thunder rumbled.

Just a shadow. Something blowing around back there.

There's no one back there. No one.

She turned away from the window with a shudder.

A loud *crack* made her jump.

"Who's there?"

No. Chill, Debra. Just chill, she scolded herself.

I'm getting as jumpy and nervous as Jenny, she thought unhappily.

There are going to be a lot of weird noises tonight, she warned herself. Tree branches falling. Trash cans being blown over by the wind. Shutters banging.

You've got to stay calm.

It wasn't easy.

For the first few weeks, this baby-sitting job had been easy. And fun. Especially since Mark sneaked over every time she stayed.

But ever since the frightening phone calls, the job wasn't fun anymore. The house had become creepy, frightening. Just *being* here was frightening.

And now Mark didn't come to help keep her company.

"Mark, where are you?" she said aloud, anger in her voice.

Impulsively, she picked up the phone and punched his number.

A sheet of bright lightning made the room seem to explode.

Listening to the phone ring at the other end, Debra's heart began to thud in her chest.

Why am I calling him? What am I going to say?

I guess I'll apologize. And ask him to come over.

I'll tell him I'm afraid. That I really need him here.

Mark's mother answered, sounding half-awake.

"Oh, I'm sorry. It's me. Debra. Did I wake you?"

Debra glanced up at the copper kitchen clock above the sink. Only eight-thirty.

"I must've dozed off in front of the tube," Mark's mother replied, clearing her throat. "I can't even remember what I was watching. Some Wall Street show on PBS, I think."

"Well, I'm really sorry," Debra repeated. "Is Mark there? I really need to talk to him."

A loud crackling on the line drowned out the reply.

"I — I can't hear you very well," Debra said, shouting over the interference on the line. "Is Mark there?"

"No. He went out," his mother said. "He isn't home."

He went out in this storm? Debra thought. Where would he go on a Monday night in the pouring rain?

"Did he say where he was going?" Debra asked. "I'd really like to reach him."

There was a pause as his mother tried to recall. "No. Sorry, Debra. He didn't tell me where he was going. Some rain, huh?"

"Yeah, sure is," Debra replied, unable to keep the disappointment from her voice.

"Should I tell Mark to call you?"

"Yes. Please. I'm at Mrs. Wagner's. He'll know. Thanks a lot. Sorry I woke you."

"Stay dry," Mark's mother said.

Debra hung up dejectedly.

She leaned against the kitchen stool, staring at the yellow-and-white wallpaper, not moving for a long moment. Then she pushed herself off, turned, and pulled a can of Coke from the refrigerator.

After two sips, she didn't want anymore. She set the can down by the sink.

Lightning flashed outside. She could hear it crack and decided it must be nearby.

Where is Mark? she asked herself.

Where could he have gone during the worst thunderstorm of the decade?

And then she had an unpleasant thought: Is he seeing someone else?

She took another sip from the Coke can. It tasted sour to her.

"Oh!" she cried as the lights flickered out.

The sudden darkness lasted only a few seconds. Then the kitchen light flashed back on and the refrigerator resumed its loud hum.

Please, *please*, don't let the electricity go out, Debra pleaded, gazing out the window into the darkness.

I couldn't *bear* it tonight if the electricity

went out and I was here, alone, in total darkness.

The phone rang loudly.

She glanced around, not recognizing the sound at first.

A second ring.

Is it Jenny? Mark?

Or is it . . .

Feeling a stab of fear, Debra's hand hesitated on the receiver.

Maybe I shouldn't answer it, she thought.

Chapter 21

The phone rang for a fourth time.

Debra swallowed hard and lifted the receiver to her ear. "Hello?"

"Hello, Marty?"

"Huh?"

"Could I talk to Marty? It's Eddie."

"Sorry. There's no Marty here," Debra replied, relieved. "You have the wrong number."

"You sure?" Eddie asked.

Debra hung up the receiver. "Yeah. I'm sure," she said aloud.

Why couldn't it have been Mark or Jenny? she wondered.

Creaking sounds from the front hall made her stop and listen.

Footsteps?

Was that a door squeaking? Someone walking quietly in the hall?

No. Just storm clouds, she told herself, not entirely convinced.

Just the house groaning. That's all.

She realized she was holding her breath. Letting it out slowly, she started toward the kitchen window. Rain pounded against the window as if trying to break in.

She was in the center of the room when the phone rang again.

This time it's Mr. Hagen.

The frightening thought broke into her mind.

This time it has to be him.

She suddenly felt cold all over.

The lights flickered again, dimmed for a moment, then came back.

The phone seemed to grow louder as it rang. And louder still, until it hurt Debra's ears.

This time it's Mr. Hagen.

Please, please — no!

She lifted the receiver to her ear with a trembling hand. "Hello?"

"Hi, Debra. It's me. Everything okay?" Mrs. Wagner asked.

"Yeah. Fine," Debra managed to choke out, her heart in her throat.

"Did the storm wake up Peter?" Debra could hear a lot of background noise. Mrs. Wagner must be calling from a pay phone, she realized.

"Peter's the best sleeper in the world," Debra said. "The storm hasn't bothered him a bit."

"Well, I'm going to be out a little later than usual," Mrs. Wagner said, shouting over the crowd noise. "Is that okay, Debra?"

"Yeah. Sure."

"I'm going to have coffee with my instructor. It shouldn't be too late. But, Debra, do me a favor?"

"What's that?"

"If I'm not home by eleven, wake up Peter and feed him, okay? There's a bottle of formula in the fridge. Just take it out, pull off the cap, and warm it up. You know how to do it, right?"

"No problem, Mrs. Wagner," Debra assured her.

"Thanks, Debra. See you later."

The line went dead.

Debra sighed. I really don't want to be here tonight, she thought. I'd rather be home.

Oh well, at least I'll make some extra money.

Carrying her Coke can, she made her way to the living room. Lightning flashed outside the large picture window. The burst of white light made all of the figurines and miniature soldiers seem to flicker to life.

Debra stopped in the doorway.

Everything in the cluttered room seemed to be moving, crawling over the tables and shelves, rolling and spinning in the flashes of white lightning.

This room is too creepy tonight, Debra decided. She removed the book she'd been reading from her backpack and quickly returned to the kitchen.

Sitting on a tall kitchen stool, resting her elbows on the kitchen counter, she concentrated on her book and tried to ignore the rumbling thunder, the hard patter of rain against the windows, and the frightening creaks and groans of the house.

At a few minutes before eleven, she looked up from her book. Formula time for Peter, she thought.

She removed the cold bottle from the refrigerator, pulled off the plastic cap, and put it in a pot of water on the stove to warm up.

I wonder how Peter will react to being awakened, she thought. Will he be cranky? Will he want his mom?

"Only one way to find out," she said aloud.

Her footsteps made the floorboards squeak as she made her way to the stairs. About to head up the stairs, she stopped — and gaped at the front door.

It was open a crack.

"Whoa!" Debra exclaimed. A cold shiver ran down her back.

I closed that door. I *know* I closed it.

One hand on the banister, she froze in place, staring hard at the door, as if waiting for it to reveal its secret.

Didn't I close it?

Didn't I push it shut and listen for it to click as I wiped my wet sneakers on the mat?

What's going *on* here?

A sudden thought eased her mind: Mrs. Wagner went out the front door to get to her car. She was in such a hurry, she probably forgot to pull the door shut.

Yes. That's the answer.

Debra eagerly convinced herself that she had solved the mystery. Feeling relieved, she pushed the door shut. Then she hurried upstairs to Peter's room.

She stopped in the doorway. The only light came from a nightlight down by the floor. It cast a triangle of dim amber light against the wall.

She stepped past the low changing table, an open box of Pampers in the corner. Past the dresser, which had several stuffed animals piled on its top.

"Peter? Time for a snack," Debra called softly.

She leaned over the crib and peered down anxiously.

"Peter?"

The crib was empty.

Chapter 22

"Peter?"

At first, Debra refused to believe her eyes.

Peter *had* to be in the crib. He *had* to be there.

"Peter?"

Squeezing the top railing of the crib with both hands, she stared down at the smooth white sheet and the light blue blanket crumpled in the corner against the wall.

"Peter?"

Why weren't her eyes cooperating? Why wasn't she seeing the baby? He *had* to be there!

Debra's hands began to shake. As her terror grew, as she began to realize that she wasn't going to see the baby in his crib, the shaking spread, until her entire body was trembling. She grasped the crib railing to hold herself up.

"Nooooooooo!"

It took her a while to realize that the long

wail of horror was coming from her own throat.

"Where *is* he?" she cried in a choked whisper. "Where? Where?"

She felt sick. She swallowed hard, trying to fight off the wave of nausea that swept over her.

"Peter?"

Without realizing what she was doing, she leaned into the crib and began pulling up the bedclothes.

She tossed the blue blanket away. "Peter?"

She pulled up the sheet. Then she grabbed up the foam mat beneath it and heaved it frantically across the room.

"Peter?"

This *can't* be happening!

Where *is* he? Where is he hiding?

Rain pattered hard against the bedroom window. A roar of thunder seemed to shake the house.

Debra stumbled blindly toward the doorway and clicked on the ceiling light.

Got to find him. Got to find him.

"Where are you?" Again, she didn't realize she was screaming.

Her eyes desperately darted around the small room.

They stopped on the dark footprint on the rug in front of the crib.

A dark, *wet* footprint on the shaggy tan carpet.

"Ohhhh." Debra sank to her knees with a low moan.

Someone was here. Someone took Peter.

Someone stole the baby.

Someone was in the house. Someone . . .

She crawled across the rug and pressed her hand on the footprint.

Still wet.

A fresh footprint.

"Noooooo!"

She forced herself to stand up. Her body felt as if it weighed a thousand pounds. She could feel the blood throbbing hard at her temples.

"What do I do?" Her eyes still raced around the room, searching, searching the dressertop, the changing table, every inch of the floor — until they rested again on the wet footprint by the crib.

"The police!"

Another powerful wave of nausea made her close her eyes. She swallowed hard. She felt hot and cold at the same time.

When she opened her eyes, the room began to tilt and sway. She pressed her palm against the wall, propelled herself forward to the doorway.

Fighting off her dizziness, she stumbled out

to the hallway. "The police. I've got to call the police."

Who did this? Who stole Peter?

Who broke into the house and took the baby?

The horrifying questions whirred through her mind as, gripping the banister, she pulled herself down the stairs.

"Ohh!" She stopped two-thirds of the way down when she saw the boy in the front entry-way.

He stared up at her with cold blue eyes.

He wore a black demin jacket over blue denim jeans, all soaked from the rain.

Debra reeled back, holding on desperately to the banister. She gaped at his short, spiky blond hair, at the red scar that ran along the bottom of his chin.

She recognized him instantly from Jenny's description.

"You — you're Cal!" she stammered. "What have you done with the baby?"

Chapter 23

Staring up at her, Cal shook his head, sending off a spray of water. He shivered. "I — I didn't mean to scare you," he said quietly.

"The baby! Where's the baby?" Debra demanded.

"Huh? I haven't seen a baby." He wiped his shoes on the mat. "I rang the doorbell several times. I thought maybe you couldn't hear me because of the rain and everything. So I came in. I'm totally soaked. I'm sorry if — "

"I don't understand!" Debra shrieked hysterically. "You don't have the baby?"

Cal's eyes narrowed on her. His expression revealed his confusion. "Baby? No. I — uh — Is Jenny here?"

"Jenny? No!" Debra screamed. She started warily down the remaining stairs. "I have to call the police!"

Cal raised his hands, surprised. "No! I'll go!

Don't call the police. Please. I'll go. I'm not a robber or anything. I was just looking for Jenny." He backed up to the door.

"You don't understand!" Debra screamed. "The baby is missing! Someone took the baby!"

"Huh?" Cal's eyes widened and his mouth dropped open as he realized why Debra was acting so panic-stricken. "Oh!" he uttered in alarm.

"Don't go!" Debra pleaded. "Stay here with me, okay? Help me."

"Yeah. Sure." Cal started to pull off his wet jacket, revealing a navy-blue T-shirt underneath.

As he tossed the jacket onto the banister, Debra hurried past him to the kitchen.

She lifted the phone receiver from the wall.

"Nine one one," she muttered to herself. "I'll call nine one one."

She held the receiver to her ear and started to push the numbers.

She stopped with a startled cry.

Silence.

The phone was dead.

Chapter 24

"What's wrong? Did you reach the police? Are they coming?" Cal asked from the kitchen doorway.

"The phone — it's dead," Debra told him, still holding the receiver limply in her hand.

He stepped into the kitchen, his eyes on the pouring rain outside the window.

"Someone took the baby and cut the phone wires," Debra said weakly.

"The phone might be dead because of the storm," Cal said.

"*Who cares? The baby's missing!*" Debra shrieked. She let the phone receiver fall to the floor and covered her face with her hands.

"I'll run next door," Cal said softly. "Maybe their phone is working."

Debra lowered her hands. "You will?"

"Yeah." He stepped toward the kitchen

door. "Sit down, okay," he told her. "Try to get yourself together."

"How *can* I?" Debra cried.

Cal pulled open the kitchen door. The sound of the rain grew louder.

"Wait!" Debra cried. "I'm coming with you."

"What for?" Cal argued. "At least one of us should stay dry. Let *me* go."

"No!" Debra hurried to catch up with him. "No, please. I don't want to stay here alone. I really don't."

Cal shrugged and pushed open the screen door.

Ducking her head, Debra followed him into the rain. Cal began to run, and she ran right behind him, slipping in the soft mud and deep puddles.

It was the crazy lady, Debra thought as the dark outline of the neighbors' house loomed ahead of them, like a giant, hulking creature.

It was Maggie. It had to be Maggie.

She said she was coming back for what was hers.

She's crazy. Crazy!

Maggie unlocked the front door, sneaked upstairs, and stole Peter.

And we'll never be able to find her because she's homeless.

She could have taken Peter anywhere!

Debra's hair was soaked. Rainwater rolled down her forehead and into her eyes as she followed Cal onto the back stoop of the neighbors' house.

Peering in through the window on the back door, she could see that the kitchen was completely dark, except for a dim light over the stove.

Cal searched for a doorbell. Not finding one, he pounded hard on the door. "Anybody home?" he shouted over the rain.

He pounded again.

Debra peered into the dim kitchen.

Cal knocked one more time. "Anyone there? Anyone?" He turned to Debra, brushing water off his eyebrows. "No one here. Next house!"

Debra leaped off the stoop and began running alongside Cal across the swampy backyard.

It wasn't Maggie. It was Mr. Hagen.

The frightening thought burst forward from the back of her mind.

He said he was coming. Mr. Hagen said he was coming soon.

Jenny tried to warn me that he was really back.

Crazy thoughts swirled in Debra's head as she ran, swirled like the wind-blown rain that drenched her. She tried to force them from her mind, to concentrate on getting to a phone and getting help.

Cal pushed his way through an opening in the tall hedge that separated the yards, sending out a cold spray of rainwater. Debra followed him through the hedge.

Gasping for breath, her temples pounding painfully, her leg muscles aching with every step, she climbed beside him onto the back porch of the next house. Stumbling over a low stack of drenched firewood logs, she pressed both hands against the wall and caught her balance.

Cal was already knocking on the door.

After a few seconds, a startled-looking middle-aged couple in matching brown bathrobes peered hesitantly out at them from the kitchen.

"Please — let us in!" Debra screamed, motioning frantically to the door. "We need help! We need the phone!"

The couple hesitated for only a moment, then pulled open the kitchen door.

"Your phone!" Debra cried, water running down her face, her hair matted flat on her head. "We need to call the police!"

The woman pointed. With a desperate gasp, Debra lurched to the phone on the kitchen table

and, blinking away rainwater, listened for a
dial tone.

Yes!

Debra pushed 911.

"Police Emergency Services," a woman's
calm voice answered after the first ring.

"Help me — *please!*" Debra cried. "*A dead
man stole the baby! Please help! A dead man
stole the baby!*"

Chapter 25

"I don't understand! I don't understand this at all!" Anger mixed with fear in Mrs. Wagner's voice. She paced back and forth across her brightly lit living room, a wadded-up tissue clenched in one hand.

Suddenly she stopped pacing and burst out in loud sobs.

A young, grim-faced policeman moved quickly across the room to comfort her.

Debra, sitting tensely on the couch, buried her head in her hands.

What a nightmare, she thought. It's a nightmare come true.

And then, with some bitterness, she thought: But it's not *my* nightmare. It's Jenny's nightmare that has come true.

She uncovered her face and gazed around the room. Cal sat beside her, his clothes soaked through, his head bowed, lost in thought. Two policemen talked together quietly by the window. A third policeman continued to comfort Mrs. Wagner, urging her quietly to take a seat in the armchair across from Debra.

Upstairs, two or three other police officers were exploring Peter's room.

The police had arrived at Mrs. Wagner's house five minutes after Debra's frantic phone call. Mrs. Wagner had returned a few minutes later, confused and frightened by all the lights and police cars.

She had reacted angrily at first, accusing Debra of being irresponsible, of letting this happen. Then, frantic with worry, she had apologized. Now she was collapsing onto the armchair in tears, sobbing loudly.

And where is Jenny? Debra wondered, clasping her cold hands together in her lap. The police had ordered the phone line repaired immediately. A repair truck had arrived within five minutes and restored the line.

Debra had called home to tell her parents what had happened. Her father was on his way over to Mrs. Wagner's now. Her mother was waiting at home — because Jenny still hadn't returned.

"I just don't believe it," Cal muttered to himself at the end of the couch. He was tapping the couch arm nervously with his open palm.

He turned to Debra. "Where could Jenny be?"

Debra shrugged. "Maybe Mr. Hagen has her, too. Maybe he's got Jenny and the baby."

Cal started to say something, but one of the police officers, leaning over Debra from behind the couch, interrupted. "I'm not sure I'm clear on what you were telling me before, Debra," he said softly, brandishing a small notepad. "Your cousin was attacked by this guy Hagen, and Hagen died? And in the past few weeks, he's been calling you and threatening to come here?"

Debra nodded. "I know it sounds crazy. But Jenny always believed he would come back from the dead. And — "

The police officer frowned and held up his free hand to stop her. "Whoa. You're stressed out, that's all. You don't really believe this guy Hagen was calling, do you? It *has* to be a cruel joke somebody is playing."

Debra stared up at him for a long moment without replying. Then she said softly, "I don't know *what* to think."

Across from Debra, hunched in the armchair, Mrs. Wagner uttered a loud sob. "If it was Maggie," she started, her shoulders heaving up and down as she cried, "if it was Maggie, we'll never find her. Never."

"Please, ma'am," a police officer said soothingly. "We'll find your baby, wherever he is."

"But she's homeless!" Mrs. Wagner declared, her voice cracking. "Homeless! We'll never find her." She shook her head miserably, dabbing at her red eyes with the wadded-up tissue. "Why didn't I change the locks?" she muttered to herself.

The police officer with the small notepad crossed in front of the couch and lowered himself onto the arm, next to Debra. "Is there anything else you can tell us that you didn't think of before? Anything at all that you remember? Did you hear footsteps or strange sounds? Did you see anything unusual?"

Debra raised her eyes to him thoughtfully. "There were strange sounds all night," she told him, "because of the storm. The house was creaking. The rain kept beating against the windows really loud."

She glanced at Cal beside her on the other end of the couch. "It — it was so noisy, I didn't hear Cal come in," she revealed.

Cal looked up. He stopped tapping the couch arm with his hand. "The front door wasn't locked," he explained, for the second time. "I just opened it and walked in."

"But why wasn't it locked? Why?" Mrs. Wagner demanded angrily, glaring at Debra.

Debra took a deep breath and started to reply. But the phone rang, startling them all.

Debra, Cal, and Mrs. Wagner leapt to their feet at the same time and started to the kitchen to answer it.

"Is it — is it the kidnapper?" Mrs. Wagner cried, trembling all over.

"Debra, why don't *you* answer it?" the police officer requested, putting a firm arm around Mrs. Wagner's shoulders to steady her. "Is there an extension I could listen in on?" he demanded.

Mrs. Wagner shook her head. "No. Only the one phone."

Debra made her way to the kitchen. Her hand hesitated over the receiver for a moment. Then, swallowing hard, she lifted it to her ear. "Hello?"

The raspy, whispered voice at the other end was familiar. *"Is that you, Debra?"*

"Y-yes," Debra stammered. She held her hand over the mouthpiece and, her eyes wide with fright, whispered to the police officer, "It's him. It's Mr. Hagen."

The police officer scowled and stepped up beside Debra, bringing his ear close to the receiver to hear, too.

"It's me, Debra," the voice rasped, dry as dead leaves. *"I got rid of Jenny — "*

"Huh? You *what*? What have you done to

Jenny? What have you done?" Debra shrieked.

"I got rid of Jenny, and I have the baby," came the frightening, whispered reply. "Now do you believe me, Babes? Now do you believe I'm really back?"

Chapter 26

Her face twisted in horror, Debra uttered a low moan.

The phone receiver fell from her hand.

The police officer swiped at it, grabbing the cord, and pulled the receiver to his ear. "Whoever you are, listen carefully," he said sternly. But then his expression changed. He slowly lowered the phone. "The creep hung up," he announced, disappointed.

"He — he said he got rid of Jenny," Debra managed to choke out. Her entire body was trembling. She grabbed the back of a kitchen stool to steady herself.

"But my baby — !" Mrs. Wagner cried. "My baby?"

"I heard Peter crying in the background," Debra told her.

"Oh, thank goodness!" Mrs. Wagner declared. "Thank goodness he's alive!"

"*What* did he say about Jenny?" Cal demanded, his face suddenly as pale as his white-blond hair.

"He said he got rid of her. That's all," Debra told him, lowering her eyes to the floor.

"What else? Did he say anything else?" the police officer demanded.

"Not really," Debra replied, shaking her head. "I heard the baby crying, and I heard — "

"Can you trace the call?" Mrs. Wagner interrupted. "How will we find my baby? How will we ever find him?"

Debra pushed herself away from the kitchen stool and turned to face the others. "I know where he is," she said, staring hard at the surprised police officer.

"Huh? What did you say?" the officer demanded.

"I know where he is," Debra repeated. "I can take you there."

Chapter 27

Debra hunched down in the backseat of the police car, watching the windshield wipers swing back and forth. Rivulets of water poured down the sides of the windshield, reflected in the lights of oncoming cars.

Debra stared straight ahead, hypnotized by the rhythmic click and scrape of the blades through dotted patterns of water, as the car, its red light flashing, burst through the sheets of rain, spraying up tall waves on both sides.

I feel like I'm on a ship, she thought. A dark, dark ship, carrying us further and further out to sea.

She sat between Cal and Mrs. Wagner, all riding in silence, all staring straight ahead. Two police officers occupied the front seats, their eyes on the twin beams of yellow light that cut through the heavy rain. Another police car, Debra knew, followed right behind.

In the darkness, houses and yards disappeared. The car swayed in the driving wind, crashed over waves on the road, making it seem to Debra as if they truly were on rolling ocean waters.

"Nice night," one of the officers muttered over the low crackle of the police radio.

"Are we almost there?" Mrs. Wagner demanded in a hoarse, trembling voice.

The officers hadn't wanted her to come, but she refused to stay home.

Moving her eyes from the hypnotic sweep of the windshield wipers, Debra glanced at Cal. He sat with his hands clasped tensely in his lap, his eyes narrowed, his features taut with worry.

"Here's the turnoff," the officer in the passenger seat instructed his partner.

Debra was thrown against Cal as the car spun off the highway, sending up a wall of water. The car bumped hard, then, with a roar, began its climb up the narrow road.

"Almost there," the driver said quietly, his eyes narrowed onto the bouncing beam of the headlights.

"But how do we know my baby is there? How do we know?" Mrs. Wagner demanded, panic revealed in the shrill trembling of her voice.

"I know I'm right," Debra told her softly.

"When Mr. Hagen was talking, I know I heard a horse whinny in the background. They've got to be at the stable. They've just *got* to be there."

"But why?" Mrs. Wagner cried. "Why would he take my baby to a stable?"

The car slid and bounced over the narrow road as it climbed. A flash of lightning surrounded them in white light, illuminating for a split second the windswept trees and tall shrubs, bending and bowing on both sides of them.

"He said he got rid of Jenny," Debra said, choking out the words. "Jenny works at the stable. Mr. Hagen must have gone there to . . . get her."

"But — but this man is *dead!*" Mrs. Wagner cried.

The officer in the passenger seat turned back to her, raising one hand, gesturing for calm. "Please, Mrs. Wagner," he said softly but firmly, "we're almost there."

"No self-respecting dead man would come out on a night like this," his partner muttered dryly, without a trace of humor. He leaned forward over the wheel, his face nearly to the windshield, and stared hard into the swirling rain.

"The stable gate is open," the other officer

said, reaching for something at his feet. "Go right through." He pulled up a large flashlight from the floor.

In the bouncing beam from the headlights, Debra could see the outline of the barn up ahead, a dark shadow against the purple sky.

"Cut the lights," the officer instructed his partner.

Now they were in complete darkness.

Debra shuddered, suddenly feeling cold all over.

Jenny, are you in there? she wondered, feeling her throat tighten with dread. *Are you and the baby in that dark barn?*

What has Mr. Hagen done to you?

Cal uttered a long sigh, but didn't say anything.

Debra knew he must be as frightened as she was.

The car rolled over the wet, muddy ground, then slid to a stop. Both officers pushed open their doors as the car came to a stop. Without saying a word, they climbed quickly out.

Behind her, Debra could hear doors slamming on the other police car.

One of the officers leaned back into the car. "Don't come out. Stay there," he ordered. "I mean it. No matter what happens, stay in the car." He slammed the door shut.

A flash of lightning illuminated the police as, hunched against the rain, they began jogging toward the dark barn. Their flashlights threw powerful beams of white halogen light ahead of them on the muddy ground.

Debra struggled to follow their progress through the rain-drenched windshield, but the glass began to steam up. Now she could see only vague shadows and shapes behind bouncing dots of white light.

"I can't just sit here!" Mrs. Wagner cried suddenly. She grabbed at the door handle. "I have to see my baby!"

"Mrs. Wagner — no!" Debra shouted.

But the panic-stricken woman pushed open the door and leapt out of the car.

"Mrs. Wagner — !" Debra called helplessly after her, watching her run through the rain, slipping in the deep mud, heading after the police officers toward the barn.

Before she realized what she was doing, Debra had scrambled out the open door. She heard Cal calling to her as she began to run after Mrs. Wagner, but she kept going.

Rain pushed her back, so cold, so heavy. Sheets of windblown rain drenched her before she had taken three steps, matted her hair against her head, nearly blinded her.

A flash of lightning illuminated Mrs. Wagner

just ahead of her, running hard, leaning into the rain with her hands outstretched as if reaching for her baby.

Beyond her, Debra could see the scrambling policemen, spread out over the muddy field, close to the barn entrance, their bright lights played over the ground.

"Is anyone in there?" A police officer's voice through an electronic megaphone rose over the pounding of the rain, the rush of the swirling winds.

"Is anyone in there? This is the police."

The bright lights were all aimed together now at the open barn doorway.

The electronic megaphone hummed loudly, then squealed, then carried the officer's stern warning: "This is the police. We have the area surrounded."

As Debra approached, breathing hard, shielding her eyes with both hands, she could see pistols drawn, revealed in the unsteady beam from the powerful flashlights.

"Is anyone in there? We're coming in!" the officer's voice carried over the roar of the rain.

"My baby! Is he in there?" Mrs. Wagner cried.

Suddenly, a flurry of movement from the barn.

Panting loudly, Debra shielded her eyes, squinting to see.

It was a horse. A horse trotting fast out of the barn, into the glare of the flashlights.

Forgetting her fear, Debra stepped closer to see. Closer.

The horse trotted out toward them, its rider sitting tall despite the downpouring rain.

Closer Debra stepped, ignoring the rain now, ignoring the mud, ignoring the thudding of her heart, staring hard at the rider on the tall horse.

"Oh!" she cried out and grabbed Cal's arm when she saw the baby held tightly in the rider's arms.

"Peter! Peter!" Mrs. Wagner was shrieking.

"I'm alive! I'm alive!" the rider called down in the hoarse, raspy voice, the voice that had filled Debra with terror over the phone.

"I'm alive, Babes! I'm back from the dead — and I'm alive!"

With a loud gasp of terror and disbelief, Debra let go of Cal. She burst past the police officers, who were too startled to stop her, and threw herself onto the side of the horse.

"Hand down the baby!" Debra cried, reaching up her hands to the saddle. "Jenny — please — hand down the baby!"

Chapter 28

In the harsh glare of the flashlights, Jenny's face appeared hard and angry. Struggling to keep the horse steady, she cradled the baby under one arm, pulling the reins tight with her other hand.

"Jenny — please!" Debra begged, reaching up to her. "Hand down the baby!"

Jenny's eyes narrowed in fury as she glared down at her cousin. *"I'm not Jenny!"* she rasped in the ugly, throaty voice. *"I'm Mr. Hagen, and I'm back!"*

"Jenny — please!" Debra pleaded.

"You didn't believe me, but I'm here!" Jenny cried. *"I'm here, and I've got my baby back! The baby-sitter killed my baby — but now I've got it back!"*

Poor Jenny, Debra thought.

Poor, poor Jenny.

"Please, give me the baby," Debra demanded again, reaching up both hands to her wild-eyed cousin.

The horse uttered a whinny of protest, bucking its head, shaking off rainwater.

Debra saw the police start to close in. She saw the glint of pistols in the bright light of the flashlights. She heard Mrs. Wagner sobbing somewhere behind her.

"Hand over the baby," the officer ordered, his voice blaring through the electronic megaphone.

Debra could feel the panic choking her as the officers moved forward in a circle. "Don't shoot her!" she screamed. "Don't shoot!"

"I'm alive! I'm back from the grave! And I have my baby!" Jenny screamed — and raised the baby high in the air, holding it in one palm. The baby thrashed its arms and legs wildly, wailing at the top of its lungs.

The officers moved forward, pistols poised.

"Don't shoot! Don't shoot!" Debra repeated.

And then she uttered a horrified scream and shut her eyes at the loud crack of gunfire.

Chapter 29

Loud sobs bursting from her throat, Debra opened her eyes in time to see the horse rear up.

Jenny slid off the saddle, still holding the wailing baby high. She hit the ground hard and collapsed on her back in the mud.

A police officer grabbed the baby with both hands and brought him close to his chest. He stepped back to hand the baby to Mrs. Wagner.

Other officers, their guns still drawn, surrounded Jenny.

"You killed her!" Debra screamed. "You killed Jenny!"

She felt Cal's hand on her quivering shoulder. But she pulled away from him and plunged past the circle of dark-uniformed police.

"Jenny! Jenny! You killed Jenny!"

Debra dropped to her knees in the cold mud beside her fallen cousin.

Jenny gazed up at her, then sat up slowly. "I fell," she said, her expression bewildered.

"But — you're shot!" Debra cried, grabbing Jenny's arm with both hands.

A police officer gently pulled Debra's hand away. "It was a crack of lightning. Close by," he told her in a low voice. "We didn't shoot. Lightning made the horse rear up, and your cousin fell."

Crouching on her knees, Debra burst into tears, tears of relief. A few seconds later, she felt someone pulling her to her feet.

"It's going to be okay now. It's going to be okay," Cal whispered soothingly. He wrapped his arms around her, trying to comfort her.

Two police officers, their flashlights circling the ground ahead of them, were guiding Jenny to a squad car. She walked willingly, staring straight ahead. In the flickering, darting light, Debra saw her dazed expression.

"Poor Jenny," she muttered, leaning against Cal. "She's so mixed up. I — I can't believe she did all those things, made those horrible phone calls, left the doll in the bushes, tried to make me believe that — "

Cal held her tighter. "Mr. Hagen *was* alive," he said sadly. "In Jenny's mind. She kept him alive by thinking about him all the time. She —

she was so obsessed by him, he finally took over her mind completely."

"If only I'd realized," Debra said sadly, walking with Cal toward the waiting police car. "If only I'd known . . ."

"You can't blame yourself," Cal said, his arm still gently around her shoulders. "I spent a lot of time with her, too. I should've seen how troubled she was."

"Well, at least now Jenny will get the help she needs. She'll be okay," Debra said, wiping away the last of her tears with the back of her hand.

"And Mr. Hagen can go back where he belongs," Cal said. "Back to the grave forever."

A police officer held open the back door of a squad car for them. Debra started to climb in, but stopped.

She raised her face to the sky.

"This really is the end of the nightmare," she said, turning back to Cal.

Cal looked up and saw it, too.

A pale half moon peeked through the clouds.

The rain had stopped.

About the Author

R.L. STINE is the author of more than one hundred books of humor, adventure, and mystery for young readers. He has written more than two dozen thrillers such as this one, all of them best-sellers.

In addition to Scholastic horror novels, he is the author of two series of scary books for young people, *Goosebumps* and *Fear Street*.

He lives in New York City with his wife, Jane, and their son, Matt.

Be warned – Point Horror has
mutated, and it's not pretty...

Andrew Matthews

Anthony
Masters

Laurence Staig

FLY-BLOWN

Philip Wooderson

Point Horror Unleashed

CALLING ALL POINT HORROR FANS!

Welcome to the new wave of fear. If you were scared before, you'll be *terrified* now...

At Gehenna's Door
Peter Beere

Transformer
Philip Gross

The Carver
Jenny Jones

House of Bones
Graham Masterton

Darker
Andrew Matthews

Blood Sinister
The Vanished
The Cunning Man
Celia Rees

The Hanging Tree
Fright Train
Paul Stewart

Catchman
Chris Wooding

Amy
Samantha Lee

Point Horror Unleashed.
It's one step beyond...